COLLIDE

CLUB PRIVÉ 11

M. S. PARKER

BELMONTE PUBLISHING, LLC

Copyright © 2016 Belmonte Publishing LLC

Published by Belmonte Publishing LLC

READING ORDER

Thank you so much for reading the Club Privé series. If you'd like to read the complete series, I recommend reading them in this order:

1. Intrigued
2. Exposed
3. Chasing Perfection
4. Craving Perfection
5. Finding Perfection
6. French Connection
7. Unlawful Attraction
8. Dangerous Attraction
9. A Legal Affair
10. A Legal Romance
11. Collide
12. Enticed

ONE
BRYNE

Okay, so maybe driving from Washington, DC to New York City during the first week of January wasn't the smartest thing I'd ever done, but since I had a history of always doing the right thing, the responsible thing, I figured I was allowed an occasional misstep.

I, however, seemed to be the only one who believed that to be true.

Right on cue, my mother's voice shouted in my head. *"You'll regret this, Bryne Dawkins. You have no clue how good you have it."*

Despite what my mother thought, I was acutely aware of how fortunate I was. I remembered what it was like before my dad died, before Mom and I moved in with Nana and Papa, her grandparents, my great grands. I remembered lying in bed and hearing my parents arguing about rent and grocery money. And I could remember walking into Nana and Papa's house, staring up at the ceiling so high above me with its glittering chandelier, unable to believe that we were going to live there now.

I wondered what Nana and Papa would've thought about what I was doing. They died shortly before I graduated high school, one of those couples who hadn't been able to live without each other. Nana had gone first – her heart – and then Papa had followed two months later in his sleep. That's when things started getting weird between Mom and me.

I sighed as I flicked my windshield wipers to high speed. It didn't do much good. The visibility still sucked, and even though it was the middle of the afternoon, it was pretty dark. I probably should have waited to move since I wasn't on any sort of timetable, but ever since I told Mom what I'd planned to do, she'd been impossible to live with. If I'd put off my plans, she would've used it as an opportunity to tell me how much I was messing up my life. Well, more than she already insisted I was.

"I can do this," I whispered to myself. I wished my voice sounded a little more solid, more like I knew what I was doing.

I risked a glance down at the GPS that was supposed to take me to the hotel where I'd made a reservation. Except nothing had changed on it since the last time I looked.

Shit.

Something was wrong with the signal. I wasn't a techie enough person to know what was wrong or how to fix it, but I did know that I was somewhere in the middle of New York City, completely lost, in a car that had been making a weird noise for the past twenty minutes.

Lost in New York.

In the snow.

In January.

At least the traffic wasn't bad. I'd been dreading that part of driving in the city. Then again, the fact that I'd only seen two cars since I'd last turned was probably a good indication that the roads weren't exactly safe at the moment.

I caught a glimpse of a bright light to my right just as my car sputtered to a stop, completing the end of a less than stellar day. I barely managed to pull it up to the curb before all forward momentum disappeared.

"No, no, no." As if the denial would actually change the fact that every light in my dash was shining like a Christmas tree.

Dammit! I slammed my hand on the steering wheel. Because, of course, that would help things.

"Come on!" I tried turning my key off, then on, but all I could hear was the clicking sound that I knew meant something had gone more sideways than usual.

Mom had tried to tell me to get a new car, but this relic was the last of my father's things. After he died and we moved, Mom had thrown out almost everything, but I'd put my foot down about the car. Nana and Papa had understood and offered to store it until I decided what I wanted to do. When I got my license, I declined their offer to buy me something new and insisted on insuring this thing. Mom told me I was being a sentimental fool, but I'd insisted.

You're so hard headed. Your stubbornness will get you in a world of trouble one day.

Today is that day, it seems. Maybe I should've listened to her after all.

I put my forehead against the steering wheel and closed my eyes, telling myself that I wouldn't cry. I was an adult dammit, and that meant I couldn't sit here on the side of the road and indulge in the tears that were burning my eyes. I had a problem, and I needed to find a solution because no one else would do it for me.

I loved my mother, but her voice had haunted me from the moment I started loading my things into my car. Now, it wasn't only her voice, but I could see her in my mind, her head shaking in disappointment.

We looked enough alike for people to comment on it. We were both short and curvy and had the same "cute" features that made us look younger than our actual ages. My eyes were from my dad though, the only feature of his that I got. Green. The same color as the leaves of a juniper tree, he always said.

Dad wouldn't have wanted me to sit here and feel sorry for myself. He'd been a boxer, and he always told me that it wasn't about how many times the other guy got in a punch, or even how often he got knocked down. What made a champion was that he kept getting back up. Not that getting back up had made my dad into one. I hadn't minded though. Things hadn't been perfect, but I'd loved my life even before I could afford anything I wanted.

It was that hard-headed nature that had given me the courage to move here by myself. Now, it would help me with my problem.

I opened my eyes and took a slow, deep breath. I needed to find out where I was before I could call a tow truck, which meant I needed to get out of the car since I couldn't see anything from where I was sitting. I zipped up my coat, grabbed my purse, and stepped out into the snow.

I quickly walked around the front so I wasn't standing in

the middle of the street, and before I'd gone more than a few steps, I was cursing the fact that I hadn't worn boots. The bottoms of my jeans were already soaked, and by the time I made it to the sidewalk, my socks were equally wet.

I really hoped this wasn't an indication as to how my new life here was going to be.

Once I was safely out of the way, I looked up, squinting against the snow as I searched for the street signs. It was no good. Between the angle and the snow, I still couldn't see much of anything.

Except the light that'd caught my attention. I could see now that it was a sign. A literal one, not some existential shit. *DeMarco's & Sons.* I hoped that the light being on meant that they were open, because I really didn't want to have to walk any farther than I had to, and I needed to find out my location.

I pushed open the door and stepped inside, blinking at the bright lights. My first impression was more sound than sight. The place was loud, and not just with the sort of noise that came with a garage. Mixed in with the sounds of tools was a radio blasting classic rock along with men's voices.

"Excuse me?"

No one even looked at me, but that wasn't surprising. I barely heard myself over the cacophony. I looked at the desk to my right and tapped the bell that was sitting there. Nothing. I scowled. I was no genius, but this didn't seem like the best way to do business.

I was starting to get warm now, and my frustration at the situation wasn't getting any better. I was tired and uncomfortable. All I wanted to do was check into my hotel room, shower, eat, and then spend the rest of the day sleeping.

I looked over at a group of four men who were the closest to me. None of them had even glanced in my direction. I sighed and started their way. I didn't know what their problem was, and I really didn't care. I just wanted to find out where I was.

Before I reached them, one of the men looked up, and I found myself staring into a pair of deep, vibrant cobalt blue eyes. They flicked down my body and then back up.

"Can I help you?"

Damn, that was some voice.

And some man, I realized, as he stood. Over six feet tall, and every inch of it lean muscle – a fact I was able to verify because he was wearing a skin tight t-shirt and a pair of worn but well-fitted jeans. His hair was dark, the color of cocoa, and tattoos wound their way up his arms, disappearing under his shirt.

I could see the desire in his eyes as I stopped, and it wasn't the soft admiration or even the sort of inappropriate lechery I'd seen before. This was soul shattering desire that made my mouth go dry and my heart race. I'd never had anyone look at me that way before, and it completely threw me. As if everything else that had happened today wasn't enough.

By now, the other three men were looking at me, but none of them held my attention like the man still watching me so intently.

"Something we can help you with?" A man to my left spoke.

I glanced at him. "I...where are we?"

"You're right here, sweetie."

All the men were standing now, and the two who hadn't

yet spoken took a step closer. The movement drew my attention, and it was only now that I realized coming in here might not have been a good idea. They were shorter than the first man – the one with the eyes – but broader, rougher looking. He looked like he could handle himself in a fight. These guys looked like they started the fights.

"My car broke down." I blurted it out before I could think better of it. "I want to call a cab, but I don't know what street we're on."

It was only as I said it that I realized I could've told a taxi to come to *DeMarco's & Sons* and I wouldn't have needed to come inside. I could've gotten back in my car and waited there. It might've been cold, but I wouldn't have felt like I was in some sort of nature documentary – the kind of documentary where an announcer with a British accent talks about how hyenas take down a gazelle who dared to stray from the pack.

And I didn't need to be a genius to know who the gazelle was in this scenario.

I wondered if I had enough time to dig in my purse for the pepper spray I bought a couple years ago. I had one of those rape whistles too, but I doubted anyone would be close enough to hear it. And judging by the way these guys looked, I doubted anyone would come, even if the thing carried sound across New York.

"I'll be happy to fix your car for you, baby." One of the other men leered at me. "And I'm sure we can work out some way for you to pay me back."

"Or you can just stay here with all of us," another man said. "You look like you could take us all on."

"I bet she'd like that."

The three of them were coming toward me, and I took a step back.

"Would you like that, sweetheart? Three fat dicks–"

"Lay off."

The words were quiet, but the three men turned toward the first man I'd seen.

"You want in on this, Dax?" The shortest of the three motioned toward me. "I'm sure she can take one more, especially one with a dick as small as yours."

The man and his two buddies laughed.

I glanced over my shoulder and tried to judge the distance to the door. Tried to remember how far it was from the door to my car. And then wondered if my car would even stop them if they were determined enough.

"Why don't you guys go fuck yourselves?" The man they called Dax said the question in such a conversational tone that it took me a minute to realize what the words actually were.

For a moment, I thought there would be a fight, but then the trio laughed again, and one of them smacked Dax's arm.

"We got shit to do," the shortest one said and threw a wink my way. "When you're done with her, try to talk her into coming back. We can have a party."

"Fuck off, Georgie." Dax walked around the three other men and came toward me, his long legs eating up the distance between us.

Electricity crackled around me, as if his very closeness changed the atmosphere of the room. I was torn between wanting to run away and wanting to know what it was like to be touched by him. Since I had no clue what the best thing to do was, I stayed in place and waited to see what he would do next.

"Dax Prevot." The words were soft, as was the small smile curving his beautifully formed lips. He held out a hand to me, and I hardly noticed the other three men walking in the opposite direction.

I placed my palm against his and felt that surge of energy I'd been anticipating and fearing. His hand was warm and strong as it closed around mine. His smile faded, and for a moment, he looked as surprised as I felt.

I'm not sure how long I stood there, drawn into the spell his presence cast over me, but it wasn't until Dax gave my hand a squeeze that I realized I hadn't offered my own name.

"Bryne," I said a bit too breathlessly for my liking, which snapped me back to reality. I pulled my hand away and gestured toward the door behind me. "If you could just tell me where I am, I'll call a taxi."

"You're in Hell's Kitchen," Dax said as he grabbed a coat from behind the desk. "Let me take a look at the car."

It wasn't really a request, I realized as I followed him outside. I shivered as the cold hit me but there was no way I was going to stay inside the shop without Dax. He was a different kind of scary than those other guys.

He didn't speak as he popped the hood of the car and started fiddling with things. After a couple minutes, he glanced up at me. "Try to start it."

I nodded as I climbed into the car, my jaw starting to ache from clenching it so tightly. I knew the moment I opened my mouth, my teeth would chatter hard enough to hurt. I breathed a prayer as I turned the key and sighed in relief when the engine turned over. It sounded rough, but it was running.

A knock at the window made me jump. Dax stood outside the passenger's side door for a moment, then opened it and climbed in without waiting for me to ask.

"Are you okay driving in this?" He didn't look at me as he asked the question. "I can drive you if you're not."

"I'm fine." I pulled my phone from my purse. "I just need directions. My GPS died."

"Where are you going?"

"Casablanca on West 43rd Street." I found myself watching him as he stared out the window. I'd always been pretty good at reading people, but this guy was impossible.

He glanced at me, then went back to watching the shop as he gave me clear, easy directions that I wouldn't need my GPS to use. When he finished, silence fell, and for a few moments, I felt like we were in our own little world.

"Thank you," I said quietly. "I don't know what would've–"

"You should be more careful," he cut me off. He turned toward me, some emotion flaring in his eyes. "Guys like that..." He shook his head and frowned. "Just be careful."

The warning didn't annoy me like it did the thousands of times I'd gotten it from my mother, which, I supposed, was unfair to her. In my defense, there was a difference hearing it from the woman who'd spent most of my life nagging me, and hearing it from a scary-hot stranger who'd essentially rescued me.

He opened the door, climbed out, then bent back down to look at me. "You're new here, right?"

I nodded. "From DC."

He seemed to be thinking about something, and I waited, hardly feeling the cold air blowing into the car.

"Meet me at Jane's tomorrow at one. It's a restaurant on West Houston Street."

He closed the door before I could even decide if I wanted to accept or decline. Apparently, that wasn't a request either. I stared at him as he walked back into the shop.

Well, damn. My new life here was definitely off to an interesting start.

Dax's directions were easy enough to follow, and I made it to my hotel without any further issues. I had a feeling I'd need to look into getting a new car soon or become a real New Yorker and use public transportation, but I wouldn't worry about that just yet. Coming here hadn't exactly been a whim, but I also hadn't planned out every single step. I was fortunate, I knew, to be able to afford to take my time to figure out what I wanted to do.

I spent the rest of the day settling into the hotel room I was going to call home for the immediate future, but after all that was done, I still couldn't quit thinking about Dax's offer. If I could call it that. It seemed more like a command. I wasn't fond of people telling me what to do, but something about him made me want to meet him, get to know him. I'd never been attracted to bad boys – and Dax Prevot definitely fit in that category – but he intrigued me, to say the least.

By the time I was in bed, trying to fall asleep, I'd decided that lunch with Dax would be the perfect way to kick things off here. I didn't want to be the same girl I was back in DC. Not that I'd go completely wild, but I wanted to start making my decisions based on what I wanted, not on what everyone would think about me.

And I wanted Dax.

I fell asleep thinking about how those eyes had stared right through me, and I was still thinking about them when I woke up the next morning.

New York was different than DC, but I was too far from being a country girl to be overwhelmed by the big city. My father had actually taught me to box a bit when I was a kid, and then when I was older, Nana and Papa had enrolled me in a self-defense class. What happened last night was foolish, but I wouldn't let it make me fearful.

Which meant I was going to lunch with Dax.

I looked the restaurant up on my phone to get directions and to make sure I had my bearings. I liked the look of it. Casual but nice. Popular enough that Dax and I wouldn't be alone. Quality food for decent prices. Good reviews. Now I just needed to decide if I wanted to risk trying to drive again or if I'd take a taxi. I didn't want to take the subway until I'd had a better chance to study the maps and make sure I knew where I was going.

The snow had stopped sometime during the night, and while there were deep drifts, the streets and sidewalks were clear enough that people and cars were out and about. The sky above was clear, and I could see enough of the city's skyline to send a thrill through me.

I tore myself away from the window and went to the dresser where I'd put my clothes. I wanted something nice, but not like I was trying too hard. Fortunately, my Nana was one of those women who always seemed to be in perfect style for every situation, and she made sure I was the same way.

I settled on a pair of nice jeans, a dark green sweater that hugged my curves, and my favorite boots. They looked good, kept my feet warm, and gave me a couple extra inches of height. At just barely five feet tall, I needed all the help I could get.

I arrived at the restaurant ten minutes early and was seated at a window table. As I waited, I found myself fidgeting. Twisting my napkin. Tapping my fingernails on the table. It was times like this that I wished I could legally order alcohol with my meal, just to take the edge off. I had a fake ID from when a group of us went to a club to celebrate our high school graduation, but it was sitting in my suitcase back in my room. Besides, I didn't think it was worth the risk just to get something to drink before Dax arrived.

"You came."

I looked up at the gruff words and saw Dax standing next to the hostess. She was openly gawking at him, and I didn't blame her. He was wearing pretty much the same thing as last night, though his jeans looked a little cleaner, but I knew that wasn't why she was staring. Dax was the kind of guy who walked into a room and demanded attention just by being there.

"I did." I gave him a small smile that I hoped masked the butterflies that suddenly took flight behind my bellybutton.

He dropped into the seat across from me and glanced over at the hostess. "Beer."

She looked startled, but when he didn't say anything else, she walked away. A few other people were shooting looks in our direction, but Dax ignored them so I followed his lead.

"I wasn't sure you'd show up," he admitted as he leaned back in his chair, that small sexy smile playing at the corner of his lips.

"I needed to eat lunch." I managed to keep my voice as nonchalant as his. "I figured since you made the suggestion, I might as well stop by. To thank you."

The corner of his mouth quirked up a little more. "Considering that I fixed your car and gave you directions, maybe you could think of a better thank you than showing up to lunch."

He raised an eyebrow and let his eyes travel down as far as the table would let him and then back up again. Slowly. I could almost feel the weight of his gaze on my body, and a flush spread across my skin. He didn't make me feel cheap or afraid, but there was nothing innocent or sweet about the way he was looking at me.

"I'll be happy to pick up the tab." I grinned at the startled expression on his face. "That is, of course, what you meant, wasn't it?"

He chuckled, a rich, deep sound that made the place between my legs ache. The smile didn't last long, turning into a scowl as our waiter approached. The woman gave Dax a once over, shrugged, and then looked at me. When her eyes dropped to my chest, I knew why she wasn't ogling the man across from me.

"Are you ready to order, or do you need a minute?" Her accent marked her as a New York native.

"I'm ready." I glanced at Dax, and he shrugged. "I'll have the grilled chicken paillard."

"Same." He didn't even bother to look at her when he said it.

The woman jotted down our orders, gave me another appreciative look, and walked away.

"Is that what you usually get?" I asked him.

He shrugged again.

I leaned forward and put my elbows on the table. "You asked me to meet you here, but you didn't bother to check the menu before you ordered. Either you don't really care what you eat, or you're enough of a regular that you know what they have."

"My cousin works in the kitchen." His eyes looked everywhere but at me. "I knew the food was good."

"Dax." I waited until his eyes met mine. "What is this?" I gestured between us.

He rubbed his hand on the back of his neck, and I couldn't help but appreciate the way the muscles in his arm flexed. "I wanted to make sure you got to your hotel safe."

I blinked. That wasn't the answer I expected, and a wave of disappointment went through me. His earlier flirting must've just been his normal way of communicating, how he naturally talked. It had nothing to do with me personally. Then again, he did just say that he wanted me to be safe.

"I did, thank you." I took a sip of the water I'd ordered.

"How long are you in town?"

It was my turn to shrug. "Depends on how things go."

He shifted in his seat, leaning forward a bit. "What things?"

I narrowed my eyes, studying him. He looked uncomfortable, like he wanted to ask me questions, but at the same time, wasn't sure how to talk to me. But that had to be in my head, because there was no way a man who looked like that had any problems talking to women.

"Why do you want to know?" I folded my arms, and his eyes fell to my breasts now pressed between them.

His gaze came back to me, locked with mine. He leaned forward, resting his forearms on the table and folding his hands together. "Because I'd like to know a little more about the woman I'll be fucking tonight."

I was pretty sure I'd heard him wrong. I must have because no one in their right mind would've said something like that to a virtual stranger. Maybe in a bar or club, but certainly not over lunch.

Except the heat in his eyes, and the smirk curling his lips told me that I'd heard him correctly, and now he was waiting to see how I'd react.

I raised an eyebrow. "You're overly sure of yourself, aren't you?"

He grinned. "Come see me at work tonight, and I'll show you why."

"I'm not going back to–" I began quickly, unable to keep the distaste from my tone.

"Not there."

Despite myself, I was curious. "Then where?"

"Club Privé." He paused while the server set our food in front of us. After the woman walked away, he continued, "I work security there. Come by tonight. Let me show you one of the fun sides of the city."

I thought about it for a moment and then came back with my own counteroffer. "If you agree to have a normal, innuendo-free lunch with me, I'll come by your club tonight."

He didn't even take the time to think about it. "Deal."

Okay then. Apparently, I was going to a club tonight. I just hoped Club Privé wouldn't look too close at my fake ID. That would be embarrassing. And since I was seriously considering following through on Dax's original presumption, getting kicked out of the club he'd invited me to wouldn't be the best way to make that happen.

I HADN'T PLANNED on going to a club the day after I arrived, but I had a couple outfits that would work. After going through them all, I wished I'd had a chance to go shopping, but in the end, I went with my favorite little black dress. I'd been told that it made me look older, which was a good thing when trying to pass for the age on my fake ID.

Since I had some skin exposed between my mid-thigh hemline and my mid-calf boots, I opted to take a taxi. Judging by the way the cab driver's eyebrows went up, Club Privé was well-known in New York, which did nothing to soothe my nerves. I pulled my phone out of my purse to see if Dax had sent me anything about how I was supposed to get in, but there was nothing. I assumed he left my name with the man at the door, and I'd just have to wait until I got through the line, but when the taxi pulled up in front of the club, there was no line.

I frowned, but paid the cab driver and got out. The man standing at the door was large, but he smiled warmly at the couple who approached him, then opened the door for them. His smile wasn't quite as wide for me, but he was definitely more pleasant than the bouncer I'd met at the club I'd gone to back in DC.

"Membership ID?"

I gave him a startled look. "*Membership* ID?"

"Club Privé is a private club for members only," he said. While he wasn't rude or even abrupt, I got the feeling this wasn't the first time he'd had to turn someone away with this explanation. "Guests have to come in with a member."

"What about an employee?"

The man gave me a hard look. "Which employee?"

"Dax Prevot."

"Are you Bryne?"

I nodded.

The man reached for the door. "Dax is working security on the floor tonight. You should be able to spot him next to the bar. Stay on the first floor. Second floor is for VIP members only."

"Thank you," I said as I hurried past him. I hadn't needed to get my ID out, so I wasn't going to risk him asking for it now.

I blinked as I stepped inside, my eyes needing a moment to adjust to the lower club lighting. It wasn't the pulsing, flashing lights I'd expected. In fact, none of this was what I'd expected. The music was danceable but not the electronic beats most clubs used. There was something sensual, silky, about it, and as I looked at the people around me, I realized why.

This wasn't just any club. It was a sex club. And based on some of the leather and chains I saw, it seemed to cater to the S&M crowd. The membership requirement made more sense now.

There didn't appear to be anything inappropriate going on as I walked toward the bar, but I had to force myself not to stare at some of the people moving around me. The clothing was as varied as the people. Some were in what I thought of as normal clubbing clothes, showing fair amounts of skin, but not unusual. Others barely had the essentials covered despite the cold outside.

"Bryne!"

I heard my name above the music and turned. Dax stepped out of the shadows, and I allowed myself a moment to appreciate how good he looked. He slid his hand up my arm and leaned in until his mouth was near my ear. Damn, he smelled good.

"You want something to drink?"

I'd told myself that I wouldn't drink tonight, if only because I wanted to keep my wits about me, but the sudden onslaught of nerves that I'd gotten the moment Dax's hand touched me made me reconsider my position.

"Nothing too strong."

Dax nodded to show he heard me and turned to the bartender. I couldn't hear what he was saying, but a minute later, he handed me a glass with something pink inside. If he'd been some random guy I'd just met, I wouldn't have taken a drink from him, but the fact that he was security here made me think that he wouldn't risk his job by slipping me a drug.

I settled onto one of the barstools and sipped my drink as

Dax moved to stand behind me. I could feel his eyes on me but kept watching the dance floor. When he leaned close enough for me to feel the heat from his body, my pussy throbbed.

I'd never had a serious boyfriend, and I'd never gone further than some hands-on action, but that had all been by choice. I'd always known that if I got involved with a man, my choice would be scrutinized to death by my mother and my great-grandparents, as well as every member of their social circle. If I was ever foolish enough to have a one-night stand, there would've been no way I could've kept it to myself.

When I first started thinking about moving to New York, dating wasn't in the forefront of my mind, but the closer my move had gotten to becoming a reality, the more I realized exactly what it would mean to be away from my mother and her expectations. I could do what I wanted to do, and my mother wouldn't know about anything unless I told her.

And there was one thing I definitely didn't want my mom to know was on my agenda. Namely, sex.

"What do you think?" Dax asked, his breath hot against my ear.

A shiver went down my spine as his fingers brushed against my back. I gulped down the rest of my drink, letting the alcohol burn its way down my throat. I was going to need some more liquid courage before I answered that question.

By the time the club closed, I'd consumed more pretty pink drinks than I cared to count, and all of my worries had faded away. The world was overly bright and a bit fuzzy, but I wasn't slurring my words, and I was completely capable of walking by myself.

That last one was the current point of contention between Dax and me.

"I don't need your help." I glared up at him as I tried to pull my arm away.

Dax grinned down at me, seeming more amused by my protests than moved by them. "I'm not letting you walk out there in those heels. You'll break your neck, and my boss will have my ass."

I made a dismissive sound. "Your boss won't fire you. Rich guys like that only care about money."

He raised an eyebrow. "Trust me, Gavin Manning isn't your average rich guy."

I stopped and stared up at Dax. "Gavin Manning is your boss?"

Someone bumped into me from behind, and I lost my balance, stumbling into Dax. His arms automatically went around me, and I found myself pressed against his chest. If I'd been completely sober, I would've immediately extricated myself and tried to play it cool, out of habit more than anything else. At the moment, however, I gave into what I wanted and wrapped my arms around his waist, breathing deeply, getting lost in the scent of soap and sweat and him.

"Bryne." Dax shifted so that I'd look up at him. His expression was serious. "How drunk are you?"

I considered the question seriously, wanting to make sure that I clearly understood what was about to happen. When I was satisfied that I could still think, I answered, "I'm sober enough to know I want you to come back to my hotel room with me tonight."

His features softened, and he lifted my chin to look directly into my eyes, desire and something else flaring hot behind his. He ran a thumb over my bottom lip and growled low in his chest.

"So beautiful," he murmured. "Unique."

The fact that he waited to answer made me even more certain that this was what I wanted. He might've had a rough exterior, but he wasn't a bad guy. My gut had been right about that. And there was definitely a connection between us.

"I'm not looking for a relationship."

I shrugged as I ran my hands around to his chest. Damn, he was firm. "Me either."

I knew there was a chance I'd regret this, but it was my choice, and that was what mattered. I'd come here to start taking control of my life, and this would be my first big step.

His eyes narrowed, and the world around us fell away. For a few seconds, all that existed was the two of us. Then he nodded and bent his head. The moment his lips touched mine, heat shot through me, and I knew I'd made the right choice. I'd had some good kisses, or at least I'd thought so at the time. Dax blew them all away.

When he finally released me, I swayed on my feet, and it had little to do with the drinks I'd consumed. My lips tingled, and my body demanded more. Any doubts I might've had about him being my first were gone. I wasn't a prude, and I hadn't been waiting for a serious relationship to come along. I'd been telling the truth when I said that I wasn't looking for anything permanent. I wanted sex, and I didn't want to settle for taking care of things myself tonight.

Dax slid his arm around my waist as he hailed a taxi. We spoke very little during the ride to my hotel, but the air around us almost seemed to crackle with electricity. I was hyper aware of every place our bodies touched, and judging by the way Dax's fingers tightened around my hip every so often, he was too.

By the time we were walking down the hallway, my nerves were stretched taut with equal parts anticipation and anxiety. I opened the door and stepped inside, wondering what I was supposed to do next.

Fortunately, Dax didn't let me wonder for long. Before the door was even closed, his mouth was on mine again. Any previous gentleness was gone as he claimed me, teeth and tongue demanding even as his hands moved over me. I managed to get my boots off, then let out a startled squeak when he lifted me up. I wrapped my legs around his waist, moaning into his mouth as he hardened against me.

I was vaguely aware that we were moving but was more concerned with the feel of his hair between my fingers, the movement of his tongue with mine. Then we were falling back onto the bed, and he released me to catch himself on his hands, his body stretched out above me.

My pulse was racing as he pushed himself up on his knees and pulled his shirt off. My breath caught as I took in the sight of him. The tattoos on his arms linked to swirls of black ink on his chest and ribcage before disappearing to his back. A small silver stud was through one nipple, and I shivered at the thought of how it must've felt to be pierced there. One of my friends back home had tried to convince me to get it done, but I'd chickened out. There was nothing chicken about this man.

"Your turn." His eyes were dark as he stared down at me.

Wiggling under him, I managed to pull my dress up and over my head, liking the way his eyes lingered on me as I slowly exposed the matching bra and panty set I'd worn underneath.

He leaned over me, his mouth taking mine again as he moved us farther up on the bed. One hand slid between us, unhooking my bra before tossing the garment aside. His hand covered my breast, his palm against the hard point of my nipple. I gasped as his fingers teased and rolled the sensitive flesh, sending pulses of pleasure through me. Then those long fingers were moving down my stomach and under my panties.

I'd touched myself before, and I'd had a couple dates who'd done some over-the-clothes groping, but I'd never had someone else's fingers between my legs. I bit down on Dax's bottom lip as a finger slid between my folds. The tip brushed against my clit, and I pushed my hips up against his hand, wanting more.

"Damn," he murmured as his mouth moved across my jaw. "So wet."

His finger slipped inside me, and I made a small sound. He pressed his lips against the side of my neck, and I closed my eyes, letting myself be lost in the sensations of his finger moving inside me, his thumb rubbing against my clit. I could feel his teeth worrying at the skin on my neck, the pull of his mouth, and I knew I'd have a mark in the morning. I might be annoyed then, but at the moment, I only wanted him to make me come. I could feel the orgasm building inside me, the way pleasure was coiling, twisting, waiting to explode.

A second finger joined the first, and now my hips were moving in time with his strokes. Then his fingers bent, moved, and I cried out as they rubbed over my g-spot. Little white dots danced across my vision, and Dax swore as I dug my nails into his shoulders. His mouth closed over my nipple, and his attentions roughened. Hard suction, sharp teeth, and the sort of pressure between my legs that told me a climax was not far off.

My muscles tightened, and I was there. I made a sound I didn't recognize, twisting my body this way and that, though I wasn't sure if I was trying to get away from Dax or trying to get closer. It didn't matter either way. He was the one in control. A second wave of pleasure washed over me, and I could barely breathe.

I wasn't even aware that Dax had moved until I heard a tearing sound and forced my eyes open. He was kneeling between my legs, his jeans pushed down to his thighs so I could see that he wasn't wearing anything underneath. As I watched, he rolled the condom over the long, thick shaft that curved up toward his stomach. My pussy clenched at the sight of it even as I realized how much bigger he was than the toy I'd packed away in one of my bags. He probably wouldn't be able to tell that I was a virgin, but it was going to be a tight fit.

He leaned over me again, pulling aside the now-soaked crotch of my panties. The rough material of his jeans rubbed against my thighs, and then the tip of him pushed against my entrance. I looked up to find him watching me closely. There was lust in his eyes, and I could feel the tension in his body, but he still took the time to make sure I still agreed to this.

I nodded, biting down on my bottom lip as he eased his way inside. As I stretched to accommodate him, I slid my hand around to his chest, needing a distraction from the nearly overwhelming sensations rippling across my nerves. My fingers found his piercing, and as I began to play with it,

Dax stilled, his body stiffening. I looked up as he growled, then cried out as he drove the rest of his cock into me with one hard thrust.

I whimpered, nails scratching at his chest, muscles trembling. I didn't know what to feel. The edge of pain that came with a deeper penetration than I'd prepared myself for. The almost unbearable fullness of being completely and totally filled. Or the pleasure from the way his body pressed into mine.

Before I was completely ready, he began to move, each stroke going deep. He wasn't being too rough, but there was no gentleness to it either. This wasn't making love or even having sex. This was fucking, pure and simple.

I wrapped my arms around his neck and began to move with him, urging him to take me harder and faster. I wanted to feel him inside me for days, wanted the memory of my first time to be branded in my mind. To be the standard against which all other encounters would be measured, even if there were no romantic feelings involved.

He shifted, the movement causing the head of his cock to drag across my g-spot with every thrust. I kept my grip on him with one hand and moved the other down between us. I moaned as my fingers touched my clit, the bundle of nerves slick and swollen. Dax's hips jerked as I clenched around him.

"Fuck."

He sounded like he was close to losing it, so I began to move my fingers over and around my clit, using the pressure and motions that I knew would get me off. His mouth closed over mine, and I parted my lips, letting his tongue mimic what his cock was doing. He slid one hand under my head, fingers tightening in my hair until it hurt.

He tore his mouth from mine. "Fucking come, Bryne. I can't hold back any longer."

He slammed into me hard enough to make me cry out, then did it again, forcing my orgasm to break over me. The pleasure was sharp, almost brutal, and I clung to Dax as he pushed himself deep, his muscles tensing. He let out a groan and pressed his face against the side of my neck.

We stayed locked together until the sensations began to ebb, and then Dax rolled off of me. I stared up at the ceiling, suddenly sober, and trying to figure out what I was supposed to do now. I was mostly naked and completely uncertain about whether or not I should cover myself or act like the nudity was no big deal.

I clearly hadn't thought this thing through as much as I thought I had.

Dax sat up, pulled off the condom and tossed it into the trashcan next to the bed. Without looking at me, he stood, pulled his pants up, and then bent to pick up his shirt.

"That was fun." He pulled his shirt over his head. "See you around, Bryne."

I watched as he walked out without a backwards glance. As the door clicked shut behind him, I wondered if I'd just made a horrible mistake.

FOUR

BRYNE

Okay, so I'd told myself that I wouldn't get all upset when the one-night stand I'd initiated was over. And I wasn't upset. Not exactly. I wasn't all weepy and wondering why Dax had walked out with barely a word. After all, he hadn't pretended this would be anything other than what it was. I wasn't angry at him or anything like that. And I wasn't really angry at myself.

I just wasn't sure if sleeping with a guy I'd just met on my second night in a new city had been the best move. Still, it had at least been my decision, made free of all the pressures that came with living in DC. It wasn't upset, I finally decided, but rather regret I was feeling, and regret I could handle.

As I finally started to fall asleep, I reminded myself that at least the sex had been good. All right, beyond good. My entire body was still humming.

When I woke up the next morning, I felt better. Yes, I'd had sex. Great, toe-curling, sex with a smoking hot guy. It hadn't been pity sex or sloppy drunken sex. It'd been two consenting adults who wanted each other. A decision I'd made for myself, and one I refused to let myself regret.

First things first though. I needed a shower. By the time I got out, I felt more prepared to figure out what I should do next. For most people who moved, getting a job would be first priority, but thanks to the inheritance I'd gotten from Nana and Papa's estate, employment was only as much of an issue as I wanted it to be.

Which meant that I could focus on the other reason I'd chosen New York City as my destination. I wanted to act, but I was hoping to make it on Broadway rather than in film or on TV, so NYC made sense. What had solidified it for me, however, was the letter my mother and I had found while going through some of Nana and Papa's things.

As I worked my brush through my hair, I paced, trying to figure out how to get the information I needed without risking seeing Dax again. I wasn't angry at him, but I didn't want him to think I was a stalker or some pitiful girl who couldn't let go. If I went back to Club Privé tonight, I was sure that's what he'd think. But I had to go back. It was the only lead I had.

My bare foot hit something, and I looked down. A wallet. I bent to pick it up even though I already knew who it belonged to. It was a sign. Now, I had good reason to go, but I wouldn't wait until tonight. The club probably wouldn't be open on a Sunday morning, but it was as good a start as any.

The bouncer wasn't there when I arrived, so I walked around the building to look for an employee entrance. I still didn't have a plan for what I'd do if no one was there, but I wasn't in a rush. As I neared the back door, however, I saw a woman coming from the opposite direction. She was a little taller than me and probably six or seven years older.

"Excuse me!" I called out as I hurried toward her. "Excuse me, do you work here?"

She looked startled, but not alarmed. "I do. How can I help you?"

"Is Gavin Manning here?"

I felt her stiffen more than I saw it, but I recognized the look in her eyes. Gavin meant something to her. The sunlight glinted off a diamond on her left hand, and intuition told me that she was married to the man I was looking for.

"Who wants to know?" she asked, her tone a little less friendly and a lot more cautious.

"My name's Bryne Dawkins." I put out a hand.

"Carrie Manning." She shook mine, but I could see that she still didn't quite know how to take me. "Why do you want to see my husband?"

I was right, and my heart gave a funny skipping beat. I'd been prepared to spend weeks searching at the very least, but instead, I'd accidentally stumbled across the person I'd come here to find.

"It's...complicated," I said, biting my lower lip, uncertain what to say or even how to begin.

A brisk wind blew through the alley, and I shivered. The expression on Carrie's face softened.

"Come on in." She swiped a card and then punched a code into the keypad next to the door. She opened it and walked inside.

I followed and found myself in a hallway rather than the open space I'd seen last night. It was dimly lit, but enough that I didn't have a problem following Carrie to a set of stairs that led up to the second floor. I remembered hearing that the upper floor was for VIPs, but Carrie didn't ask me to wait, so I went after her.

We stopped in front of a door, and she knocked, opening the door a moment later. When I stepped inside after her, she moved to the side so I could see the man sitting behind the desk. Dark hair, deep blue eyes. His features weren't familiar, and for a moment, I doubted that he was who I'd come to find, but I'd never know if I didn't speak up.

"Gavin, someone's here to see you." Carrie took off her coat, and I saw that she was pregnant. Probably four or five months. Her winter coat had hidden it. Her hand automatically moved to her stomach as she turned, the gesture protective.

Gavin gave me a puzzled look, but that was no surprise. Even if he knew of my mother's existence, I doubted he'd known of mine. He stood. "Can I help you?"

"I'm Bryne Dawkins." Straightforward was probably the best way to go with this, but I had a feeling it would come as quite a shock however I worded it. "I'm your niece."

Gavin's eyes widened, and he looked from me to Carrie and back again. "Say again?"

"I think I'm your niece," I clarified my statement. "Is your father's name Chauncey Manning?" At his nod, I continued, "And he worked at the US Embassy in Sweden like thirty years ago?"

"Yes." He gestured to the chair across from him. Carrie moved to lean against him, and he took her hand. "But I'm still lost."

I sat down and took a deep breath. "My mother's name is

Allison, and her parents were Nancy Lyons...and Chauncey Manning."

Gavin gave his head a little shake. "I'll need a little more than a couple names here, Bryne. My parents never said anything about a half-sister."

I reached into my pocket and pulled out both of the things I'd brought with me. The wallet I set on the desk. The letter, I held out to Gavin.

"After my dad died, my mom and I went to live with my great-grandparents. A few months ago, we were cleaning some things out of an old desk, and we found this letter. Your dad wrote it to my grandmother about thirty years ago. In it, he says that he met someone in Sweden, that they married and had a son. Gavin."

He unfolded the letter and began to read, so I shut my mouth and let him. For me, this wasn't really a shock. I'd never known my grandfather. Hell, I'd barely known my grandmother, and my memories of her weren't fond ones.

After a couple minutes, he folded the letter back up and held it out to me. When he looked up at me, his expression was unreadable. "I believe you, but I think I'd like a couple minutes to call my dad. He has some explaining to do."

I nodded and stood. Completely understandable. I glanced down at the desk and saw Dax's wallet. I gestured toward it. "By the way, that belongs to one of your employees. Dax Prevot."

One eyebrow went up, and something flashed across Gavin's eyes. "May I ask why you have Dax's wallet?"

"Gavin." There was a note of amusement in Carrie's voice.

I folded my arms and gave him a hard look. "I'm an adult."

One corner of Gavin's mouth twitched. "Barely."

Carrie smacked his arm. "You've just met the girl. I think it's a bit early to be going all alpha male on her."

"Stay away from Dax," Gavin said, his gaze fixed on me.

I wasn't entirely sure how to take him, but I'd never been one to shy away from asking questions. "Why?"

"Some of his acquaintances aren't exactly the most trust-worthy of people," Gavin said. He glanced at Carrie, who seemed to want to say something, and then added, "And he's not exactly known for his fidelity."

I rolled my eyes. "If I was looking for a boyfriend, that might be an issue."

I wasn't going to let myself think about how nice it might be to go to bed with Dax again. I would probably have some other one-night stands, some casual relationships, but my time with Dax was done. I wouldn't go there again.

Carrie broke the silence before it could become uncom-fortable. "Bryne, why don't you and I give Gavin some time alone to make his phone call. If he wants to play overprotec-tive uncle, he can do it later."

We walked toward the door, and I glanced over my shoul-der. Gavin's eyes were fixed on Carrie, and I felt a sharp, painful longing. I'd never been one of those girls who spent time on romantic daydreams, but in that moment, I wanted someone to look at me the way Gavin was looking at Carrie.

"So, Bryne," Carrie said as we walked into the hallway, "where are you staying?"

FIVE

BRYNE

The only thing my newfound uncle told me about his conversation with his father was that I was right, and we were related. I didn't press the issue. If he and my mom wanted to go into detail about their childhood, and the ways their father had screwed them both over, that was between them. I hadn't come to find Gavin for some sort of closure.

I wanted family.

Considering I was staring up at the same ceiling for the third morning in a row, I was pretty sure I'd found it. As soon as I told Carrie that I was staying in a hotel until I could find somewhere more permanent, she'd insisted that I move into the guest room in their loft. I told her that I could afford to stay in a hotel for a while, but when she told Gavin, he made it clear that it was pointless to argue.

I supposed I could've shown them both just how stubborn I was, but if I was completely honest, I didn't want to argue. I liked Carrie and Gavin, and I wanted to get to know them. I'd loved Nana and Papa, and I loved my mother, but I'd always been a little sad about the fact that I didn't have any extended family. The kids from the families who ran in the same social circles as my great-grandparents weren't exactly the friendliest to the daughter of a dead boxer.

Carrie and Gavin were older than me, but not so much that I felt like I had parents hovering. Sure, Gavin was a bit overprotective – he'd stuck to his insistence that I needed to stay away from Dax – but he wasn't condescending about it, so I didn't take offense.

By the time I made my way into the kitchen, I could smell coffee and knew that Gavin and Carrie would be waiting. Since I'd moved in, we'd eaten breakfast together every morning. Because Gavin ran Club Privé, and Carrie had her own law practice, they more or less set their own hours unless they had an appointment scheduled, so we were spending most mornings together. It was a nice combination of getting to know them without being overwhelmed.

"Krissy called," Carrie said as soon as I came over to the table with my mug of hazelnut coffee.

A flare of hope shot through me, but I kept my expression neutral. When I told Carrie and Gavin that I wanted to pursue a career in acting, I'd expected the same brush off that I'd gotten from my mother and teachers back home. Instead, Gavin had told me to let him know if I wanted any help finding a job that would be willing to work around an acting schedule until I landed a full-time gig, and Carrie had offered to contact one of her closest friends, who apparently ran a talent agency in Los Angeles.

"That was quick," I said as I sat down across from her.

"When Krissy gets something in her head, she doesn't let go until she gets what she wants." The amusement on

Carrie's face told me that she was thinking of something specific. "Anyway, she gave me a couple names and some casting calls that you might want to check out." She pushed a piece of paper across the table.

"Thank you so much," I said. "Seriously, I can't thank you both enough."

"It's what family does," Carrie said.

I skimmed the list, my heart skipping a beat when I saw that one of the casting calls was this afternoon. "This is really happening."

Carrie smiled at me as she reached across the table to squeeze my hand. "As soon as you're done, come by the club and tell us how it went."

"You're sure that's okay?" I glanced at Gavin.

He'd made it clear that he didn't want me at Club Privé, but it hadn't just been him being protective. If word got out that a nineteen-year-old had been drinking in his club, he'd lose his liquor license and possibly even the club itself. He'd given the bartender, bouncer, and Dax all warnings that the next time they didn't check an ID, they'd be fired.

I'd gotten the impression that the warning to Dax was as much about staying away from me as it had been about being diligent regarding keeping people under twenty-one from drinking.

"Come in the service entrance," Gavin said. "Either Carrie or I should be in the office."

A few minutes of silence followed his statement, and then I broke it. "Can I ask you a question?"

He glanced up from his tablet and nodded.

"Your parents met in Sweden, right?"

"Yes."

I hadn't done much questioning about Gavin's past, but I was curious. "How did you end up in New York?"

Gavin straightened so that he could give me his full attention. "My dad's job changed, so he moved us all back here. He worked in New York, but after a couple of months, my mom said she didn't like living in the city. They bought a house in Stamford, Connecticut, and my time was pretty much split between the two. I went to school in Stamford, though, so I consider that my home."

"And that's where your daughter lives?"

He nodded but didn't elaborate. He didn't need to. I'd gotten enough from Carrie to know not to ask for details. Skylar lived with her maternal grandparents, and though Gavin saw her as much as possible, he hadn't wanted to take her away from the people who'd raised her after her mother died. According to Carrie, Gavin had been too broken up over the death of his childhood sweetheart, Camille, to raise a child and had given custody to Camille's parents.

Some people would see Gavin's actions as someone shirking their responsibility, but even after just a few days, I knew that wasn't the case. Gavin was the type of man who would do what was right for the people he loved, no matter the cost to himself.

I supposed that was why his warnings about Dax didn't make me mad. I knew Gavin's heart was in the right place.

I didn't ask any other questions as we finished our breakfast. I needed to focus on the audition. It wasn't a huge Broadway production, a new play called *Collide*, but it would be a foot in the door, and that's all I really wanted. I didn't have a problem with a little assistance, especially in a world where who a person knew was sometimes more important than their abilities, but I refused to be one of those people who bought or ass-kissed their way into something rather than earning it.

My stomach was in knots when I walked into the room after waiting in line for nearly an hour. The trio of people sitting behind the table in front of me looked completely unenthused at the prospect of yet another actress coming in to read for them, which didn't help matters, but I wouldn't let it keep me from trying.

For the longest two seconds of my life, I was afraid I'd throw up if I opened my mouth, but then I started to talk, and everything else faded away. I'd auditioned for dozens of roles back home – and gotten a little more than half of them – and even though this production was only a little bigger than any of the ones I'd done in DC, knowing that I was in New York, not that far from Broadway, somehow made it different.

I walked out of the room fifteen minutes later and felt like I was walking on air. I'd nailed it. Of course, the two women and one man who'd been listening to me hadn't said much more than *thank you* and explained that they'd be making their decision by the end of the week regarding callbacks, but I knew in my gut that I'd been good.

And I was pretty sure I'd seen the one woman crack a smile.

Even if I didn't get the part, I felt better knowing that I could do this. I'd made it through an audition without breaking down, vomiting, or forgetting my lines. That was one of the things I'd been worried about. I never considered myself susceptible to stage fright, but I knew there was a first time for everything. This time, at least, hadn't been it. And I hadn't been told that I was hopeless either, so that was a plus too.

I had the taxi drop me off in front of the club, but I bypassed the front door and headed around back. It was still early enough that the front doors were locked, but even if they'd been open, I'd promised to come in through the side entrance. I didn't want to do anything to get Gavin and Carrie into trouble, not when they'd done so much for me already.

I swiped the card and punched in the code Carrie had given me, then headed toward the stairs and back up to Gavin's office. The door was closed this time, but the light was on inside, so I knocked. I heard movement, a muttered curse, and then the door opened.

Carrie's face was flushed, her curls disheveled. If that hadn't been enough to tell me that I'd interrupted a...*personal* moment, the annoyed expression on Gavin's face as he appeared behind her would've done it. The look only lasted a moment after he saw me, then it disappeared behind a smile.

"You look like things went well," he said as he motioned for me to come in.

"I think they did." I felt a little awkward, knowing they'd been getting down – hot and heavy if Carrie was any indication – until I'd coitus interrupted them, but I was pretty sure it would be worse if I actually acknowledged it. Granted, the two of them ran a sex club, but that didn't make it any less weird to talk about any of that with them.

"When should you hear if you got it?" Carrie asked.

"They'll decide callbacks by the end of the week."

She gave me an encouraging smile. "I'm sure they'll ask you to come in again."

I didn't want to get my hopes up, but I couldn't stop myself from smiling. "Even if they don't, make sure you tell your friend that I really appreciated her telling me about the audition."

"If you ever decide you want to head out to LA, I'll give you her information." Carrie glanced over at Gavin. "But tonight, we're going to celebrate."

I raised an eyebrow. "Celebrate what? All I did was audition. We should save the celebrating until I actually get a part."

"I think we should be celebrating your start of a new life here," she said, her brown eyes shining. "I'm meeting with two of my friends, Dena and Leslie, for dinner. You should come with me."

"She's underage," Gavin said quietly.

Carrie glared at him, but even I could see how much she completely adored him. "Don't tell me that, Gavin. You'll ruin my super-secret plan to ply your innocent little niece with alcohol and corrupt her."

He rolled his eyes while I laughed under my breath.

"Seriously, Bryne, I think you'll like Dena and Leslie. They're great."

It wasn't like I had anything else planned. The only person other than Carrie and Gavin that I'd spoken more than a couple words to was Dax, and I hadn't seen him since he'd walked out of my hotel room.

"Sure. What time should I be ready?"

SIX

BRYNE

The first thing I noticed when I walked into the restaurant was that I'd seen one of Carrie's friends before but couldn't figure out where. She was a good half foot taller than me, with brilliant red curls and a confidence that was evident even from across the room.

The second thing I noticed was that Carrie made a face as she took the seat next to the red-head, like sitting down was uncomfortable. Before I could ask about it though, Carrie was making introductions.

"Bryne, this is Leslie Calvin and Dena Monroe."

I hadn't even noticed the other one until now. She was tiny, with short white blonde hair, and a fierce expression that told me it would be a bad idea to mess with her.

"Girls, this is Bryne Dawkins."

"Gavin's niece," Leslie said. She tilted her head and narrowed her eyes, studying me for a moment before speaking again. "You don't look like him much. Probably a good thing. He'd make an ugly woman." She shrugged and then raised her hand to flag down a waiter.

"Don't mind Leslie. She basically says the first thing that pops into her head, whether she should or not." Carrie tossed a sugar packet at Leslie.

Leslie caught it and tossed it back. "Somebody has to say it."

I laughed. I hadn't had any close friends growing up, but this was how I'd always imagined it would be. Easy camaraderie, being able to say whatever I wanted without fear of judgment.

"Behave yourself," Carrie said. "Gavin'll be pissed if you guys scare Bryne away."

I gave her a startled look. While Gavin was nice and we'd talked, I hadn't gotten the impression that he felt that strongly about me. After all, he hadn't even known of my existence a week ago.

"Gavin's not always the best at showing how he really feels, but he feels deeply," Carrie murmured, her hand stroking my arm.

"She's right," Leslie said, turning to me with that bright smile.

It suddenly clicked where I'd seen her before. "You're engaged to Paxton Gorham."

As soon as I said it, I wanted to take it back. I was sure she got a lot of crazies wanting to talk to her because she was engaged to one of the hottest rock musicians out there. I'd never been one of those kinds of people who fawned all over celebrities, and I didn't intend to be mistaken for one now.

"Damn straight I am." She held out her left hand so that the diamond caught the light. "Man's all mine."

Dena and Carrie rolled their eyes, but I leaned down to look more closely at the ring.

"It's beautiful," I offered. "You're a lucky woman."

"I am." Her smile softened as she looked down at the ring. "Paxton's amazing, and so's Carter." She looked up at me, her expression serious. "I never thought I'd settle down and get married, much less be a stepmom, but I wouldn't trade my family for anything."

"Carter's a great kid," Carrie agreed. Her hand moved over her stomach. "Skylar's been asking when they can play together again."

"Gavin and Paxton are going to have their hands full with those two," Dena said.

Leslie nodded. "Paxton's already figuring out he can't pull any of that alpha male shit with Carter, and I'll bet Gavin knows it too." She looked at Dena. "You just wait. Arik'll find out pretty quick that his whole Dom thing won't work on a kid who wraps him around her little finger."

"Leslie," Carrie hissed. Her cheeks flushed as she shot a glance my way.

"Come on, Carrie," Leslie said. "You guys run a sex club. I'm sure Bryne's figured out that..." Her voice trailed off for a moment. "Shit. Oops."

Alpha male.

Dom.

Sex club.

Shit.

Heat flooded my face. I may have been a virgin before coming to New York, but I hadn't been a nun. I knew what all those things added up to.

"Are you guys telling me..." I looked at each of the

women who were all blushing various shades of pink and red. "Well, damn."

Carrie pointed a finger at Leslie. "This is your fault, and don't think I won't throw your ass to the wolves the second Gavin finds out you're the one who told his niece about our sex lives."

I stared at them as they laughed. It was one thing to read about stuff like this in magazines and books, or to have theoretical discussions. It was something else entirely to be talking with three professional women who were actually living the life. These women were lawyers with established careers, and based on what I was hearing, their significant others were something out of a romance novel.

The really dirty kind that included whips and ball-gags.

Something clicked, and I turned toward Carrie. "You winced when you sat down. Was that from..." I couldn't figure out the best way to finish the question, so I let it dangle in the air.

Dena chuckled. "Punishment or play?"

Carrie glared at her friend. "None of your damn business."

Leslie's laugh was loud, but not obnoxious. "That means it was punishment. What'd you do?"

I couldn't believe the conversation going on around me. They were teasing each other, but it was clear there was no shame or humiliation in it. I had no idea how they'd gotten into this lifestyle, but they apparently loved it.

And I wanted to know more.

So for the next couple hours, we talked about sex more matter-of-factly than I ever had before. They told me how each of them had come to be involved in BDSM, how they'd decided what their own preferences were. They talked about terms like Dom and Sub and Switch, and what they really meant. The true nature of those sorts of relationships. I almost felt like I was back in school, trying to memorize terms and definitions, except the subject matter was *nothing* like what I'd learned in school. Sex Ed had made most of my classmates giggle and blush, but it wasn't even comparable to the conversation I was a part of. Even without alcohol, by the time we were done, my head was spinning.

"So," Carrie began as we headed for the door, "did we completely freak you out?"

"No, but it was definitely different." I zipped up my coat and followed her outside.

There'd been a question hovering in the back of my mind, refusing to leave, no matter how much noise everything else was causing. A part of me wanted to say that it didn't matter what answer Carrie gave, that it wouldn't change anything, but I still couldn't stop thinking about it.

So I gave in and asked, "Does everyone who works at Club Privé...are they all into the whole BDSM thing?"

Carrie gave me a sideways glance as a town car pulled up to the curb. "This wouldn't happen to have anything to do with a certain club employee whose wallet I returned earlier this week, would it?"

My cheeks burned. "Maybe."

She grinned and climbed into the back. The driver was different than the one who'd taken us to the club, but he still greeted Carrie by name. Apparently, Gavin wasn't just a club owner, but a successful entrepreneur in a variety of ways, including running a car service. He'd offered me the use of it free of charge, something I'd forgotten on my way to the audition. Nana and Papa had employed a couple drivers, but I'd only used them for special events. I'd always preferred to drive myself.

Not that I intended to do much of that here. Aside from the fact that I was pretty sure my car was about to give up the ghost, until I knew the city better, I didn't intend to experiment with navigating myself.

"Is the whole S&M thing the reason Gavin told me to stay away from Dax?" I blurted out the question, then glanced toward the front of the car, wishing I'd been a little more discreet.

"Don't worry about him," Carrie said. "The window between us is soundproof. Once he rolls it up, we have to use the intercom to talk."

I relaxed a little bit more into the seat and looked expectantly at Carrie as I waited for an answer to my question.

"That's part of it," she finally said.

"Seems a bit hypocritical," I pointed out.

One side of her mouth tipped up in a partial smile. "Have you ever noticed, that when it comes to members of their family, men are often that way?"

I shrugged. "I wouldn't know. I never really had the chance to learn."

She reached over and squeezed my hand. "Gavin really is trying to look out for you."

"So you think Dax is a bad guy too?"

She paused, clearly thinking about what she was going to say. Finally, she shook her head. "Not exactly. Gavin was right in that some of the people Dax spends time with aren't exactly the nicest people."

I nodded, remembering the other guys who'd been in the

shop that first night. I wasn't one to judge by appearance, but my gut told me those guys had earned any reputation that followed them.

Still, there was something about Dax.

"And the women?" I tried to keep my tone casual, but the look in Carrie's eyes told me that I wasn't fooling her.

"He does have a bit of a reputation as the kind of man who isn't interested in the long-term." She squeezed my hand again. "But there's more to him than that. Without going into details, I can say that Dax will do anything for the people he cares about, and I think, for the right woman, he'd change his ways."

I nodded but didn't say anything. I didn't have anything *to* say. My brain felt like it was on overload trying to sort out everything that'd happened in the past few days. I knew I shouldn't even be considering having anything more to do with Dax, and not only because of the warnings Gavin had given me. The career path I'd chosen wasn't an easy one, and I should focus on it. Get myself into a couple shows and find a place of my own. Once I was solid, then I could think about romance.

Besides, Dax said he didn't want a relationship.

A little voice in the back of my head said that maybe that was a good thing. Maybe I didn't have to worry about all those questions. Dax hadn't said he didn't want to see me again. He said he'd enjoyed himself, and that he'd see me around. Maybe the answer to everything was a happy medium. I enjoyed spending time with Carrie and Gavin, but it'd be nice to have someone else to hang out with, to go do things with.

Friendship wasn't a relationship. Not like the one Dax

had said he didn't want. Hell, maybe we could throw in some benefits and get the advantage of having sex without the headache that came with having a boyfriend.

I wanted to sleep on the idea, but maybe I'd feel the same way in the morning. If I did, then I'd have a little trip to make after Gavin and Carrie went to work.

The weather hadn't gotten any warmer, though we hadn't had another snowstorm since the night I'd first arrived, but the sun was bright enough to hurt my eyes as I got out of my car and stood in front of *DeMarco's & Sons*. Idly, I wondered about the grammatical correctness of the sign but knew I was only stalling.

I wanted to see Dax again, more than I truly felt comfortable admitting, even to myself. I'd reminded myself repeatedly that I'd had plenty of male friends back home, and this was no different. True, none of them were close friends, and I hadn't wanted to sleep with any of them, but I was determined to make this work. Carrie seemed to think Dax was a decent guy, so I'd take her word for it.

I took a slow, steady breath, rubbed my sweating palms on my jeans, and stepped inside.

Like the first night I'd been here, the noise hit me before anything else. It was louder than before, with more people working and moving about. No one was behind the desk, so I took a moment to look around. The table where Dax and his friends had sat was empty, but I spotted one of the guys working on a massive motorcycle. Pretty much everyone was working on motorcycles, and since I couldn't tell one from another, it all pretty much looked the same.

"Can I help you?"

I recognized the voice before I turned. Dax had called him Georgie, and I'd hoped to avoid seeing him again. I refused to let him chase me away though, so I steeled my nerves and turned back toward the desk.

"Good morning." I kept my voice as even as possible.

His dark eyes narrowed, then lit up with a recognition I didn't like. "I know you, sweetheart." He winked at me. "Decided you liked what you saw after all?"

I refused to take the bait. "I'm looking for Dax."

He grinned, not taking his eyes off me as he called out, "Yo, Dax. Girl here wants you. Guess you're better with your dick than I thought you were."

My mouth flattened into a tight line. Gavin hadn't been wrong about Dax's friends being assholes.

"What are you yelling...?" Dax stopped talking the moment his eyes met mine.

For a split second, I thought I saw a flash of something – lust or longing, I wasn't sure – but then it was gone. Dax's gaze hardened, his expression morphing into something I didn't recognize.

"Hey, babe." The same sort of smarmy grin Georgie was wearing curved Dax's mouth. "You need something?" His eyes took a slow journey down my body.

I should've left. Everything in me was telling me to leave. But I'd never been one to take the easy way out.

"I wanted to talk to you." I kept my eyes on Dax, waiting for the man who'd stuck up for me the last time I'd been in here.

He shrugged and leaned on the counter. "So talk."

I hadn't expected an audience, so I blurted out the first thing that popped into my mind. "Did you get your wallet back?"

He laughed, but it wasn't a nice sound. "Yeah, I got it. How'd you manage to get it to the boss?"

"He's my uncle."

That got a reaction. "No fucking way." He laughed again. "I guess if I couldn't fuck the boss's daughter, the niece is the next best thing."

My face burned as Georgie laughed too. I could feel the eyes of the men behind us as their attention shifted toward me.

"So you did get a piece of that ass." Georgie didn't stop leering at me while he spoke to Dax. "Damn."

I ignored Georgie and glared at Dax. He raised an eyebrow and crossed his arms, almost like he was daring me to say something.

"How good was she?"

Out of the corner of my eye, I saw Georgie take a step toward me.

"Maybe I should take her for a spin."

A muscle in Dax's jaw clenched, another small bit of genuine reaction. "Don't bother." He looked away from me. "It's not worth the hassle."

I felt sick to my stomach, but beyond any of the hurt I felt was anger. Anger that burned deeper than anything I'd felt since my mother told me that my father was dead.

"You're a miserable son of a bitch, you know that?" I was proud to hear that my voice didn't waver.

"Hey, I told you that I didn't do relationships." He shrugged. "Not my fault you came looking for seconds."

"That's not why I'm here, asshole," I snapped. "Carrie told me you were a decent guy, and I thought that she might be right. Apparently, she's not as good of a judge of character as she thought. You're a fucking bastard."

"She talk like that in bed?" Georgie asked. "I don't like them mouthy bitches."

I finally turned toward him. "I don't give a damn what you like because I'll never touch you." I looked back at Dax and jabbed a finger at him. "And I'm sorry I ever let you touch me. A mistake I don't intend to ever make again."

I walked away before I could give in to my urge to punch him in the nose. My hands were still clenched into fists as I walked outside. I was glad I'd driven rather than taking a cab or a town car. I wouldn't have wanted to wait around. At some point, I was sure I'd cry, if only because I was pissed, but I wasn't there yet. No, if I'd had to wait for a ride, I probably would've been tempted to throw something heavy.

Probably at his crotch.

The concentration it took to drive in Manhattan traffic was good for one thing. It forced me to focus on what I was doing, and not on how much I hoped the next woman who slept with Dax gave him syphilis.

By the time I let myself into the loft, however, the anger at Dax was starting to turn into anger at myself. I'd wanted so much to be my own person that I'd rushed into a decision that I should've thought through. If it'd only been Dax leaving right after sex, that would have been one thing, but the way

Dax had just behaved...Carrie wasn't the only one who'd misjudged him.

"Bryne?"

Carrie's voice drew me out of my head.

"Are you okay?"

I wanted to smile and say that everything was fine, but the kindness in her voice after how rude Dax had been was too much. I shook my head and felt the first pricking of tears against my eyelids.

"Come here." She put her arm around my shoulders and led me over to the kitchen table. "Now, you tell me what's wrong and whose ass I have to kick."

EIGHT

BRYNE

After talking to Carrie and taking a hot shower, I felt better. As much as I sometimes complained about her, my mother and I didn't have a bad relationship, but we also didn't have the sort of close mother-daughter bond that allowed us to talk easily about personal things, especially now. Even though I'd only known Carrie for less than a week, I felt much more comfortable talking to her than I would have to my mother. I supposed her having shared about her own sexual preferences made it easier to talk to her about what happened with Dax. That and the fact that she didn't act like I'd done something wrong helped me come to terms with the whole thing.

By the time Carrie left to meet Gavin at the club, I was already moving on to the things that really mattered, the things that I should have been focusing on instead of Dax. I needed to decide whether or not I wanted to buy a new car, and what to do with the old one if I did. I also had to decide if I wanted to find a place of my own before I found a job or after. While I still hoped that I'd get a call tomorrow saying that I was wanted for a callback, I knew I couldn't count on it. The odds were better than if I were trying to get on Broadway, but they were still low.

I knew that, technically, I had enough money to live comfortably without needing to work, even if I continued to pay for my mother to live her life in Washington. I was sure most people in my situation would be happy pursuing their dreams without having to worry about making money, and I didn't necessarily think there was anything wrong with that, but it wasn't what I wanted. I wanted to use as little of my inheritance as possible so that it would be there if I ever really needed it. Like if or when I had a family.

Not that I was thinking about having a family anytime soon. I clearly needed to work on my taste in men quite a bit more before I even considered anything serious. I could only imagine what would've happened if I'd been careless when I slept with Dax. The last thing I wanted was to have a baby with an asshole like that. I planned on being much smarter when it came to sexual partners in the future. No way would I make the same mistake twice.

In fact, I decided, I'd swear off men completely until I had a solid plan and was at least a few weeks into it. I didn't need distractions. With that in mind, I pulled out my favorite notepad and got to work. A bit of spontaneity wasn't bad, but if I was going to succeed, I couldn't just wait for things to fall in my lap.

I was so engrossed in what I was doing that the buzzer rang twice before I realized that the doorman was trying to get my attention. I walked over to the speaker, pulling my robe more tightly around me.

"This is Bryne," I announced.

"Miss Dawkins, there's a young man down here who says that he needs to speak with you."

My stomach flipped. I only knew of one young man who might want to talk to me, but I wasn't sure I wanted to talk with him. I knew I should though, if for no other reason than to not be the petty person that a refusal would paint me to be.

"It's okay. Send him up."

I considered running to my room and throwing on some clothes, then decided against it. I wasn't sitting around eating ice cream and weeping. I was having a night in while planning for my future, and there was no dress code for that. I wasn't going to let Dax dictate my appearance.

I stayed near the door and refused the urge to try to do something more with my hair than the braid it was currently in. When he knocked, I took a slow breath, counted to ten, and then opened the door.

The expression on Dax's face told me that he wasn't here to apologize. A part of me wanted to take a step backward, but I gripped the doorframe and held my ground.

"It's bad enough you had to be a clingy little bitch but getting me fired is going too far."

I blinked, unsure of which part of his accusation I wanted to address first. "What are you talking about?"

His eyes were dark, but not the way they had been the night we slept together. No, this was pure fury glaring down at me. "Don't play dumb. I might not have gone to some rich boarding school like you did, but I'm not stupid."

I straightened and folded my arms, biting back the smart replies I wanted to give. I'd let him say whatever he wanted and then tell him how far off-base he was. If he wanted to make a scene, it would be his reputation that got trashed, not mine.

"I told you I wasn't looking for a relationship. Then, when I don't call you after I go back to your hotel like you begged me to, you come to my work and get all upset when I don't kiss your ass. That's bad enough."

It was on the tip of my tongue to tell him that he was full of himself, but I didn't.

"Then you had to go crying to your uncle and get me fired."

Gavin fired him? I hadn't told Gavin anything about what happened between Dax and me. "I didn't—"

"You're a real bitch, you know that?" Dax cut me off. "I'm not like you. I work my ass off at two jobs so I can take care of my mom. Gavin and Carrie helped me with her, but now that you had to open your big mouth and lie about me, all that's changed."

My self-control reached its limit. "Shut. The fuck. Up."

Surprise flashed across his face, then disappeared. He opened his mouth, but I wasn't interested in listening anymore.

"You had your turn. It's mine now." I glared up at him. "First of all, I didn't come to the shop to try to get you in bed again or because I wanted to be your girlfriend, you're dead wrong about that. Since I was new here, I thought I'd take a chance that you were actually a decent guy I could be friends with. I never would've had sex with you if I'd known you were a lecherous asshole."

He stared at me, those eyes blazing into mine before falling to my lips. He shook his head, as if trying to clear it, and ran a hand through his hair before scrubbing both hands over his face. "Whatever the reason, it still doesn't give you the right to get your uncle to fire me."

I held up my hand. "I'm not done." I poked him in the chest, and his hand shot up, capturing my fingers in his grasp. "You don't know me or much of anything about me, so let me make this perfectly clear. I didn't tell my uncle anything. He knows we slept together because I had your wallet, but that was just him figuring it out. I didn't tell him I went to talk to you, or that you were an utter bastard. I don't know why he fired you, and I really don't care. If you want to know so badly, grow a pair and talk to Gavin yourself."

I tried to yank my hand away, but his vice like grip only tightened. His face twisted with an emotion that resembled pain, but was gone so quickly I could have imagined it.

He finally let go of my hand and I slammed the door shut. "Bryne!"

"Go away, Dax!" I shouted through the door. "Don't make me call security!"

When I didn't hear anything else, I walked over to the couch, my legs feeling like lead. I sat down and put my head in my hands. If Dax had come in to apologize for his behavior, explaining it as him being an ass because of his friends, I might've forgiven him, maybe even still wanted to be friends with him. If he'd told me before about working two jobs so he could take care of his mother, I would've been impressed.

None of that matter now though. He'd shown himself for who he truly was. A temperamental child who cared only about what people could do for him. It was funny how people usually thought of spoiled brats as coming from rich, indulgent families, and I'd known enough of those to know there was a grain of truth in that stereotype. The thing most people didn't know or didn't want to admit was that it was less about money and more about entitlement. Clearly, the chip on Dax's shoulder told him that the world owed him something, and he didn't like it when things didn't go his way.

Fuck him.

I'd had enough. If I thought I'd waver on my *no men* resolution, Dax had reinforced just how important that was. From here on out, I would focus on work and the new members of my family. I'd chalk Dax up as a mistake to learn from, and move on.

NINE

BRYNE

Going off on Dax made me feel better funny enough. I finished writing out my long-term goals, as well as what steps I needed to take to reach those goals. I'd always been the sort of person who, if I vented about what was bothering me, I could put it to the back of my mind. I didn't stew about things, and I tried not to hold on to them. I much rather preferred to forget about things I couldn't fix, problems I couldn't solve. Life was too short to spend worrying about what I couldn't control.

I slept better than I had since I moved, and when I woke up, I was ready to start on my list. My stomach growled. After I had some breakfast. It smelled like someone was making bacon.

"Hey, Bryne," Carrie said as I entered the kitchen. "How'd you sleep?"

"Good," I said as I retrieved a plate from the cabinet beside the stove. I leaned against the counter. "Did you say anything to Gavin about me being upset with Dax?"

Okay, so maybe I hadn't completely forgotten about it, but I told myself that it was natural to be curious about what happened with Dax's job. He may have been a jerk to me, but I didn't like the idea of him losing his job because my uncle was being overprotective.

Carrie's cheeks went pink. "Um, no."

My eyes narrowed as a thought occurred to me. Dax hadn't actually said that Gavin had personally fired him. Gavin was the boss, so it was natural to assume that he'd been the one calling the shots.

"Did *you* fire Dax because of what I told you?"

When she finally looked at me, there was a stubborn set to her jaw. "Yes."

I sighed. "Really? Gavin doing it, I guess I could see, but you, Carrie? I didn't think you were that overprotective."

"I'm not." She went back to pushing bacon around with her spatula. "Don't get me wrong, I wanted to cut off his balls for the way he talked to you, but I'd never make a business decision based on personal feelings."

I raised an eyebrow. "Then why'd you fire him?"

"I never told you how Dax got hired, did I?" She glanced at me, and I shook my head. "I mostly work on human trafficking cases, but sometimes I take on other cases that spark my interest. A year ago, a former client referred a case to me where a woman was injured at work, and her company fired her."

I recalled a comment Dax had made last night. "Dax's mom."

Carrie nodded. "Annabeth didn't deserve what happened to her. I've been working on her case, but the company was trying to drag things out rather than settle. Gavin and I offered Dax a job so he could help his mother."

"But you fired him." I was completely confused now.

"I did," Carrie said. "And it was because of what he said to you, though not for the reason you think."

I snatched a piece of bacon and ate it while she continued.

"Most people look at Club Privé as a sordid place where people go to have kinky sex." She gave me a partial grin. "While I suppose that's technically true, the club is more than that. It's a place where people with common interests can come and not worry about what other people think about them. We rely on trust and respect." Her expression grew serious. "Someone who would behave so disrespectfully to a woman he'd had sex with can't be trusted to maintain the sort of discretion and respect needed to work in that sort of setting. *That* is why I fired him."

My respect for Carrie went up even more. Before I could say anything though, my phone rang.

"Hello?"

"May I speak with Bryne Dawkins?" The woman's voice was pleasant, but she pronounced my name wrong, making the *y* sound like a long *i* rather than a short one.

I didn't bother to correct her. "Speaking."

"This is Jacqueline Jamison, the casting director for *Collide*."

My heart felt like it lodged in my throat.

"We'd like you to come in for a second reading for the part of Gretchen."

Gretchen. The romantic lead.

"Th that would be great." I found the closest chair and sat down. "When do you want me to come in?"

"Would it be possible for you to come in this afternoon? Four o'clock?"

"Yes, I can be there."

"Great. We'll see you then."

I stared at my phone for a solid minute, unable to believe what just happened.

"Bryne?" Carrie touched my hand.

"I have a callback." Hearing it still didn't make it feel any more real.

Carrie threw her arms around me. "That's wonderful! Tell me all about it!"

THE FACT that I'd gotten a callback on my first New York audition should have meant I'd be more relaxed going in for a second audition but, if anything, I was even more anxious. I wasn't expecting to get the part. Rejections were a part of wanting to be an actor. I'd prepared for that. Even if I didn't get the role, I hadn't prepared to get this far so fast.

It was stupid, I knew, to be so thrown by something good, but that didn't do anything to keep my pulse from racing and my mouth from going dry. I took a quick swig from my bottle of water and then told myself that if I wanted to be an actress, this was a good place to start. If I couldn't convince them that I wasn't nervous, then I didn't deserve the job.

"Miss Dawkins." Jacqueline smiled at me when I entered the room. "Today, you'll be reading with Todd Emery. He'll be playing the lead character, Christopher Halloway."

I hadn't noticed the new person in the room until now. About six feet tall, unruly strawberry blond hair, and a gorgeous pair of smokey gray eyes, Todd was perfect for the role of the broody romantic lead. He smiled at me and stepped forward, stretching out his hand.

"Bryne Dawkins," I said with a smile.

"All right, Miss Dawkins," Jacqueline said. "We'll have you and Mr. Emery read a scene, see what the chemistry is between the two of you."

I nodded and accepted the page the director handed me.

Twenty minutes later, Todd took me in his arms and bent his head to give me a scorching kiss. It was a good kiss, the kind that would read well onstage but wasn't too intrusive. The perfect way to end the scene.

When we both turned to the table, all three faces were beaming at us.

"That was great," Jacqueline said. "Seriously, Bryne, the best we've seen."

She said my name correctly this time. I hoped that, plus the praise, meant good things.

"What do you think, Todd?" The director looked at the man standing next to me.

"She's my choice," he said without hesitating.

"Mine too," Jacqueline added.

All eyes turned to the third person at the table, the one who hadn't spoken yet. She nodded as well.

"Technically, we have to go over some things before we can make an official announcement." The director stood, a smile on his face. "But I think, unofficially, we can agree that you're our choice."

"Congratulations." Jacqueline came around to shake my

hand, but I could barely process what she was saying or doing. My head was buzzing.

I shook her hand, then the other two as well. I was barely aware of them leaving, and then I was alone with Todd.

"Did that really happen?" I asked, looking up at him. "Did that seriously just happen?"

He grinned at me, a brilliant smile that made him look even more handsome. "I'm guessing this is your first gig."

I nodded, then shook my head. "Not exactly. It's my first one here in New York. I did some stuff back in DC, but this is...different."

He chuckled, a nice, warm sound. "Tell me about it. I grew up doing theater in Boise."

"How long have you been here?" I asked.

"Eight years this spring. And I wouldn't go back for the world. It's not always easy, and sometimes we have to deal with some shit people, but if you love it, really love it, it's worth it."

I smiled, the tension in me finally easing. Here was someone who got it, who really understood what it meant to want to be a part of something like this. I'd been wrong to go looking for a friend in Dax. We had nothing in common. Here was where I'd find like-minded people, people I could be friends with.

I wasn't stupid. I knew there'd be backstabbing and jealousy, people who'd be petty and cruel. But there'd also be those who knew what it was like to work long, grueling hours while outsiders talked about how nice it must be not to really have to work for a living. People who understood having to work shit jobs to pay the bills, then going to rehearsals and performances. Getting by on only a couple hours of sleep. Forcing a smile or laugh when every inch hurt.

"We should do something," Todd said. "It's the first leading role for both of us. We should celebrate before we have to fill every waking hour with practices and performances."

I looked up into those kind eyes of his and thought about that kiss. There hadn't been a spark with him, no real heat. Sure, it'd been for an audition, but I didn't really feel anything now either, looking at him. Admiration, yes. Even a bit of physical attraction, but no real desire. I didn't care if he touched me or not. I had no real opinion about whether or not he kissed me.

"What do you think?" He reached out and twisted a loose curl around his finger. "Dinner. Maybe a drink."

I took half a step back. "Right now?"

Todd smiled at me. "We can go later if you have someone you want to invite. My boyfriend's visiting his parents in Miami, or I'd invite him along too."

Boyfriend.

Todd was gay. Well, maybe bisexual, but at the very least, he was taken. I didn't have to worry about him hitting on me or taking things the wrong way. I could just hang out with him, spend time with him. We could do things together, and I'd never have to worry about it becoming weird and awkward.

I smiled at him. "That sounds great. I'm starving."

TEN

BRYNE

"This place is amazing. How'd you find out about it?" I couldn't stop looking around, not even when the waiter placed the most amazing smelling pasta in front of me.

"Hiram's cousin owns the place," Todd said as he speared another piece of zucchini. "She's one of my favorite people."

Hiram was Todd's boyfriend of three and a half years. According to Todd, Hiram was the whole package. A gorgeous, accomplished architect, he was also in his mid-fifties and had two daughters around Todd's age. Apparently, he'd been married for twelve years before finally coming out. He and his ex-wife were still friends, and his daughters absolutely loved Todd. Once a year, they all took a vacation to the Catskills together.

By the time we'd ordered our main courses, I knew more about Hiram than I did my own father. Todd loved to talk, and his favorite topic of conversation was his boyfriend. I didn't mind though. I was more than happy to take the time to listen while I enjoyed my meal.

"So, Bryne Dawkins," Todd said after he finished a story about the first time he'd met Hiram's youngest daughter. "How do you like the Big Apple so far?"

I shrugged. "It's different than DC, especially without my mom here."

"Do you have any family here at all?"

I laughed, and Todd gave me a puzzled look. "That's a crazy story."

He pointed his fork at me. "Spill. I live for crazy stories."

"Okay, so the short version is that my mother found out just a couple of months ago that she has a younger half-brother. She never knew her father, but we found this letter from him talking about how he went to Sweden and met this woman. They got married and had a son, but he never told them about my mother. When it turned out that my uncle lived in New York, I decided that I'd come here to pursue acting and meet him."

"You just showed up on this guy's doorstep like 'hey, I'm your niece?'"

"Pretty much." I sipped at the wine Todd had ordered. "Though it was stranger than that how I even ended up meeting him. When I first got here, I met this guy who told me to come see him at work, and he works security at this club."

Dax's face popped up in my mind. Not the angry, cruel version of him I'd seen, but the way he'd looked the first night, and the night we slept together. A real smile on his face, eyes sparkling, then dark with desire.

I pushed those thoughts away. Dwelling on the past wouldn't do anyone any good.

I continued my story, focusing on the part with Gavin

rather than Dax. "While I'm at the club, this guy mentions the name of his boss. I was a little tipsy, so I didn't really register it until the next morning. It turns out that my uncle owns the club I was at."

"Which club?"

I hesitated. I knew that Carrie had said that they were discreet, but I wasn't sure how far that went. They'd have to advertise somehow. Then again, if the only way to get in was through a member, maybe they relied on word of mouth.

"Club Privé."

Todd's eyebrows shot up, telling me that he knew exactly what sort of club it was. "Your uncle is Gavin Manning?"

"You've heard of him." I made it a statement rather than a question.

"Yeah, he was in the news a while back. He and this lawyer were responsible for bringing down a human trafficking ring that was doing business through the club."

"Didn't it tie into a hit and run from almost ten years ago?" I asked. "I remember hearing about it."

Todd nodded. "The victim was his girlfriend or fiancée. She was even pregnant at the time. Didn't your uncle tell you any of this?"

I shook my head. "He told me that he had a daughter and that her mother had died, but nothing else." I leaned back in my seat. "Wow. I had no idea. I mean, I knew Carrie works on those sorts of cases, and that they make sure there isn't anything illegal going on at the club, but they never told me why."

"I'm sure it's not something they really want to think too much about," Todd offered. "From what I remember, there was a lot that didn't even make the news, just spread around from person to person. I'm not sure how much of it is true, but if it is, I'm sure that's why they don't talk about it."

Curiosity piqued, I asked, "What did you hear?"

Todd leaned closer and lowered his voice. "The guy who was running the whole thing, he tried to kidnap and sell the woman lawyer. Some people say he tried to rape her. No one really knows how bad things got. Only that there were injuries and that the cops found a whole lot of nasty shit when they searched the guy's place."

I was silent, letting it all sink in. I already liked Carrie and Gavin, but hearing how they put their lives on the line to stop something that awful made me think even better of them. Nana and Papa would've liked them. I wasn't sure if that meant my mother would, but at least I could tell her that they were good people.

Eventually.

I hadn't told her I'd planned to look for her half-brother. Considering how angry she'd been at me for leaving, I'd known that would only make things worse. I wanted to know more about Gavin before I decided to tell her about him. If he was some creep, all it would've done was make her more upset at the whole situation. Now, however, I could at least feel justified in pressing her to meet him.

"So, that woman lawyer, do you know what happened to her?"

I grinned as Todd's question pulled me out of my thoughts. "He married her, actually."

"Is that the Carrie woman you mentioned before?"

I nodded. "She's really great."

"They must've kept her name out of the papers to prevent

anyone from coming after her. It was a gutsy thing they did." The admiration in his voice was clear.

"It was," I agreed.

"Are you ready for dessert?" The waiter smiled down at us.

I shook my head and looked at Todd.

"Just the check," he said.

"Two checks," I corrected.

"One," Todd insisted. He looked at me. "Dinner's my treat."

"Okay," I agreed, but held up a finger. "But only if we get some drinks, and those are my treat."

"Deal."

"Taxi or subway?" Todd asked as he handed the waiter a credit card.

We'd walked here from the callback, but I definitely didn't feel like walking now. I pulled my phone out. "I've got something better."

"What's better?"

"Wait and see," I said as I opened the app. Gavin had three town cars that were specifically on call for him and family. The one that had dropped me off at the callback was only a couple minutes out.

As we walked outside ten minutes later, it was already dark, and the temperature had dropped a few degrees, making me glad we weren't walking. I shivered and pulled my coat more tightly around me. The sleek black town car was waiting at the curb.

"There's our ride," I said, gesturing at the car.

"Seriously?" Todd gave me a searching look. "You're not like some senator's secret love child, are you?"

A laugh bubbled out of me. "No, I'm not. My uncle has a town car service and an app."

I got into the backseat and waited for Todd to slide in next to me.

"Where to, Miss Dawkins?" The driver glanced in the rearview mirror.

I looked at Todd.

"Club Privé?" His eyebrows went up and down.

I remembered Gavin's warning about not getting him into trouble. But then I reasoned that if I didn't drink, then technically, I wouldn't be breaking any laws. And I'd already had a glass of wine, so I was okay with not having anything else.

"Club Privé," I repeated to the driver. "But take us to the employee entrance."

Todd shot me a questioning look.

"Sneaking in through the back?" Todd said.

I chuckled and shook my head. "We're not going to sneak. We'll go in the back way so I can tell Gavin that I'm there. And besides, this way we can skip the line."

The ride from the restaurant to the club wasn't very long, and as we bypassed the front door, I saw a handful of people heading inside. It was a Friday night, so I had no doubt the place would be packed.

Once we were at the back door, Todd politely looked away as I ran the keycard and punched in the code. I grabbed his hand and pulled him after me as we went inside. It was nice to be able to hold his hand and not have to worry about him reading anything into it.

I started to lead the way to the stairs when I saw that Gavin was already coming down them. His eyes narrowed when he saw me, but I knew he wasn't really annoyed until he spotted Todd behind me.

"Hey, Gavin." I gave him a bright smile. "This is Todd."

"I thought we had this talk." Gavin glowered at Todd and then down at me. "You're not old enough to be in here during club hours, Bryne."

"I didn't go in through the front," I said, giving him an imploring look.

He raised an eyebrow. "That really doesn't make it any better."

"I came in this way so I could tell you that I was here. I don't want to drink. All I want is to blow off some steam."

"With him?"

"Todd Emery." Todd stepped around me and held out his hand. "I'm in a play with Bryne."

"Really?"

Todd grinned. "And I'm gay...and I have a boyfriend."

Gavin smiled. "I like you better already."

"I had a feeling that would help." Todd chuckled.

Gavin turned to me. "That doesn't mean I like the idea of you being here."

"I just want to dance. I promise, no drinking."

"I'll keep an eye on her," Todd said. "Water only for both of us, and I'll make sure she gets home safe."

After a few moments of silence, Gavin nodded. "All right, but if anything goes sideways, it'll be your ass."

Todd's expression was serious. "I don't doubt it."

Gavin gave me a hard look. "Go. Have fun."

Todd slid his arm around my waist as we walked out into the main room. It was different, coming in this time and knowing what to expect. Knowing that there'd be men and women in leather and chains, in barely-there clothes, made it easier not to stare when we walked past.

The trio of people performing on stage, however, were a little harder to ignore. Two men and one woman. The men were strapped to a pair of crosses – the X kind – and the woman behind them was wielding a pair of floggers, alternating blows to their already pink skin. Judging by the way their erections were tenting their pants, they were thoroughly enjoying themselves.

About half of the people in the club were watching the action on stage, but the other half were on the dance floor, and it was in that direction that Todd took me. We went right past the bar, and I was tempted to glance that way even though I knew Dax wasn't here. The gentle pressure on my hip, however, kept me moving, and then Todd was turning toward me, and I focused on him.

He pulled me close, one hand on either hip, and I draped an arm over his shoulder. It took less than three beats for the two of us to fall in sync with each other. One song blended into another, and my world became rhythm and sound. The feel of Todd's body moving against mine, the literal heat between us. It was good, solid, fun without the confusion of sexual attraction.

Dancing with Todd told me that we'd be great together on stage. We had chemistry, and we could make the audience believe that we were in love. I was willing to bet that half of the people dancing around us thought we were together, and we weren't even trying.

My job was solid at the moment.

I was having a blast with Todd, and I was willing to bet

that the two of us would become great friends. He would be a part of the new life I planned to build here.

I could do this. Hell, I was doing it.

I had a feeling, despite my bumpy start, I was going to like New York.

ELEVEN
BRYNE

After nearly tow hours of blowing off steam on the dance floor, we both settled in one of the couches, exhausted.

"You're a great dancer," Todd said as he handed me a bottle of water.

"Thank you." I took a long drink, letting the cool liquid slide down my throat before speaking again. "You're great too."

"Don't get me wrong, I love Hiram, but I miss dancing."

"Hiram doesn't dance?" I leaned closer to Todd, so I didn't have to shout as loud.

He shook his head. "I got him to slow dance once or twice at a wedding, but that's about it. He claims he has no rhythm." Todd bent closer and grinned. "He's right."

I chuckled and drained the rest of my water. "Well, if you ever want to blow off more steam on the dance floor, I'm available. As long as Hiram doesn't mind."

Todd waved a hand. "If anything, he'll be grateful that I

found someone else to go with. He's not the possessive type." He slung his arm around my shoulders. "He'll love you."

The fact that he assumed I'd be meeting his boyfriend made me smile. "I'm sure I'll love him too."

"You ready to go, or do you want to stay a while longer?"

I considered it for a moment but then reminded myself that Gavin was already pushing things by letting me be in the club at all.

"I should probably get going." I gave him a smile. "You can stay though. Have some fun."

Todd shook his head. "Aside from the fact that being at a sex club alone when one's boyfriend is out of town isn't a good idea, I promised your uncle that I'd make sure you got home safe."

"I don't think he meant for you to literally take me home."

Todd shrugged. "It's the least I could do for getting into one of the most exclusive clubs in the city for free."

"You really don't have to," I argued.

"I'm doing it," he said firmly. "Let's go."

After the heat of the club, the winter air was extra frosty, but it felt good against my cheeks. I should've been exhausted after my long day, but I wasn't. If anything, the dancing had woken me up, and now the cold air energized me. Todd might've been taking me home, but I knew I wouldn't be getting to sleep anytime soon.

"So," I asked as we started down the sidewalk, "was the club everything you thought it would be?"

"More," Todd said as we passed the line of taxis parked out front. "I mean, I'm not really into the whole BDSM scene, but I'd have been crazy not to take advantage of getting to see the inside of Club Privé."

"That's my ride right there." I pointed at the car a few feet farther down the sidewalk. "He's one of Gavin's drivers, so we can drop you off first, and then he can take me home."

"We can argue semantics once we get out of the cold," Todd said as he reached for the back door.

"That didn't take very long."

I froze mid-step as a far too familiar voice cut into the conversation. I glanced up at Todd and saw him looking over my head. Shit, I hadn't imagined the voice. I forced a tight smile onto my face and turned.

Dax pushed himself off the wall and sauntered toward us, his hands stuffed into his pockets. The expression on his face was frostier than the ice that had suddenly surrounded my heart.

I folded my arms and tried not to let him see how much I really didn't want to be doing this. "Dax, this is Todd. Todd, Dax."

Dax gave him a once over, then clearly dismissed him. "You going to get him fired too? Or does he not work for your uncle?"

"Bryne?" Todd put his hand on my elbow.

"Let's go, Todd." I started to turn, but a tight grip on my upper arm stopped me. I glared up at the owner. "Hands off, Dax."

Todd stiffened next to me, but Dax let me go before I had to worry about any macho displays of testosterone.

"It's okay," I said, keeping my eyes on my new friend.

"Who's he?" Todd's expression was full of concern.

"The guy who got to her before you."

I rolled my eyes. "You're an ass, Dax."

Todd looked from me to Dax and back again. "I think the two of you have some...issues to work out."

"We really don't," I said. "It's all been worked out."

Todd looked at Dax, then gave me a knowing smile. "Honey, trust me. You two need to talk. I'll get a taxi."

"Take the car," I insisted. "I'll call another one."

He shook his head. "Not a chance. I promised I'd make sure you were safe. If you're taking one of your uncle's cars after your talk, the driver will make sure you get in safely. I'll take a taxi." He glared over at Dax. "And if anything happens to her, I'll make sure Gavin knows exactly who she was with."

Todd leaned down and kissed my cheek before walking away.

I sighed and turned toward Dax. If he thought I was taking a single step away from this car, he was nuts. We'd have it out here, then I'd get in the car and go home. Well, Gavin and Carrie's home. Not DC home.

"Say whatever it is you need to say, Dax. It's cold out here."

His eyes narrowed, and he took a step toward me. I'd almost forgotten how tall he was. How broad his shoulders were. The long, lean length of...shit. I seriously needed to stop.

"I originally came here to apologize." He glowered down at me. "But now I see I was just interrupting your latest hook-up. Don't let me stop you if you want to go after him."

"Do whatever you want, Dax. I don't care."

"Like hell you don't." He took another step toward me, closing the distance between us until hardly any remained. "You want me."

"I don't." I spoke through gritted teeth, determined not to be the first to back down.

His gaze held mine for several long beats, and I could feel the tension between us building. Before I could decide what I wanted to do about it, his hands closed around my arms, and he yanked me toward him. His mouth came down on mine in a fierce, bruising kiss.

I knew I should shove him away. I didn't want to be kissing him. At least, my brain didn't want to be. My body, however, was yearning to be even closer. Electricity hummed along my nerves, the interior heat chasing away the exterior cold. No matter how stupid I knew it was to be kissing him back, I couldn't bring myself to pull away.

One arm slid around my waist, pulling me tight against his body. He buried his free hand in my hair, his tongue stroking across my lips until they parted. I clutched the front of his coat, hating myself even as I clung to him. When he finally broke the kiss, my breath came in pants, and it was all I could do to stay standing.

Then I looked up at him and saw the smug expression on his face.

"I think that counts as wanting me."

I shoved at his chest, catching him off guard enough to make him take a couple steps back. "If you kiss me again without my permission, I'll knee you in the balls."

The smirk hardened. "Don't worry, sweetheart. I won't be doing that again. Just wanted to show you what you'll be missing with pretty-boy."

"First off, Dax, who I spend my time with is none of your business. You made it perfectly clear that what happened between us was only a one-time thing. In fact, I believe we agreed that neither one of us were looking for a relationship. Jealousy isn't a pretty color on you."

"I'm not jealous."

I raised an eyebrow but didn't argue. "Second, Todd has a boyfriend, asshole."

I turned and reached for the door handle. Suddenly, Dax's arms were around me, pinning me against the car. The front door opened, and the driver stepped out.

"I suggest you unhand Mr. Manning's niece." The tone was hard and demanding.

"It's all right," I said. "Dax won't do anything stupid. Will you?"

"Naw. I always think things through."

I waited until the driver got back into the car before I eased myself back around to look up at him. "Don't make me regret not asking him to kick your ass, because I'm pretty sure he could take you."

His eyes dropped to my mouth. "Why didn't you?"

"Because I'm an idiot."

He leaned into me. "Somehow, I don't think that's the reason."

"Well, since you apparently know everything, why don't you tell me? And don't say that I want you. I want chocolate cake for breakfast. It doesn't mean I'm dumb enough to eat it."

Something very much like triumph flared in his eyes. "So you do want me."

I blew out an angry breath. "It's cold and I'm tired, Dax. Say whatever it is you want to say so we can go our separate ways."

"What if I don't want to go separate ways?"

I rubbed my forehead. "First, you say you don't want a

relationship. Then you act like a complete ass when I just wanted to talk about being friends. *Then*, to top it all off, you accuse me of getting you fired. What the hell are you going on about?"

Dax's hands came up to cup my face, his palms hot against my cold skin. "I did say and do all of that." His eyes drifted down to my lips again. "Fuck, Bryne. You have no idea how badly I want to kiss you."

He bent his head, but I put a finger on his lips. "Talk only. You haven't earned permission to kiss me again." I shifted my weight so that I was able to bring my knee up to brush against his thigh, reminding him of my previous threat.

"That night, the minute we finished, I wanted to be inside you again." His voice was rough. "So I left. But I couldn't stop thinking about you. When you walked into the shop, I knew it'd be easier to push you away than admit how much I wanted you."

I swallowed hard. This couldn't be real. He couldn't be telling me all of this because this was what I so badly wanted to hear. What the dull ache inside me had been waiting for. I wanted him to tell me that I meant something to him, even if only physically, and even that seemed like too much to hope for.

"And now?" The question came out in a whisper. "How do you feel now?"

"Like all I want to do is bury my face between your legs and lick you until you scream my name. Fuck you until you can't think. Take you for hours, until all you can breathe and feel is me."

His gaze burned into me, telling me the truth of everything he said.

The smart thing would be to tell him that we needed to take things slow. That he had to earn my trust, make up for the things he'd said.

But I didn't want any of that.

I wanted him in all the ways he said he wanted me.

This wasn't a proposal or even him asking for a date. This wasn't the way a relationship started, wasn't the way to make something lasting.

But it was what I wanted.

I grabbed onto the front of his shirt, made my decision, and then said, "Kiss me."

TWELVE

BRYNE

Despite the way Dax's kisses made my head spin, I still had enough sense to ask the driver to take us to a hotel. While I fully intended to let Gavin and Carrie know where I was, I wasn't about to bring Dax into their home without talking to them about it first. And right now, I wanted as few delays as possible.

Dax's hand slid higher up the inside of my thigh, pushing my legs apart, causing me to type out a jumble of letters that weren't even a word.

"Dax," I practically moaned his name as his lips traced along my jaw. "I need to finish this text."

"Go right ahead," he murmured, his breath hot against my skin. "You're not bothering me."

I put my hand on his chest, fully intending to be firm and push him away, but then his fingers skimmed the crotch of my panties, and I shivered, my fingers curling into his shirt.

He made a sound of approval as his mouth touched the rapidly fluttering pulse in my throat. "If just a few kisses got you that wet, then I plan to have you soaked by the time we get to the hotel."

"I…"

His teeth grazed my skin, and I forgot what I needed to say. Then his fingers pressed against me through black lace, and I forgot to care about what I was supposed to be doing. Forgot that we were in the back of a car. My hips moved against his hand, wanting more.

"What do you want, Bryne?"

I hadn't realized I'd closed my eyes until I had to force them open to look at him. "I…I want to finish my text so that we're not interrupted at the hotel."

The smile that curved his lips couldn't be called anything other than dangerous. "Are you sure that's really what you want?"

A finger stroked my skin just under the elastic of my panties.

Damn him and the way my body responded to his touch.

"You have a choice here," he continued. "I can take my hands off you, and not touch you again until we're in a room so you can finish what you're doing, or you can see how much you can get done while I get you off."

I gulped in a hitching breath. "Are you sure you aren't a member of Club Privé? You seem to like being bossy."

He chuckled, then leaned forward to bite at my bottom lip. Not enough to cause real pain, but enough to make me gasp. "I never said I wasn't into all that." He moved his mouth to my ear. "Do you want me to show you?"

I nodded before I'd even fully processed the question.

"Then pick up your phone."

My hand was shaking as I reached for my phone, but it

wasn't fear or even anxiety. It was desire, pure and simple. If anything about desire could be simple.

"Finish telling your uncle and aunt that you're safe."

His fingers moved under the damp fabric, over the thin layer of curls.

How the hell was I supposed to think with his hand up my skirt?

"Finish that text, Bryne, or I stop."

His tone was firm, confident. If he said it, he'd do it.

I tapped out the remaining few words, struggling to process a coherent thought as a finger slid inside me. My head fell back, a moan escaping before I could stop it.

"Finish."

I hit send. "Done."

"Good girl." He began to move his finger in short, shallow strokes, just enough to keep me wet, but not enough to give me what I needed.

My phone alerted me to a text. I glanced down and saw that Carrie had responded for the both of them. I was sure she'd ask more questions tomorrow, but she wasn't asking them now. Another text came through even as Dax pushed a second finger inside me.

"Todd." Dax practically growled the name. "Tell him you're fine."

I gasped as he twisted his fingers, his easy motions turning rough. His free hand went to my hair, pulling it free of the messy up-do it'd been in. He wrapped my hair around his hand and held me tight as his fingers moved inside me. My eyes locked with his, and I saw no anger, no malice in their depths. A hint of jealousy mingled with lust, but I knew I was safe with him.

I picked up my phone and tapped the microphone. "I'm fine, Todd." I bit my lip to keep from crying out as Dax's thumb pressed down on my clit. My voice shook as I continued, "Gavin and Carrie know where I am. I'll talk to you later."

I sent the message just as Dax curled his fingers to rub against my g-spot. My back arched, muscles tensing with the strain of staying quiet. I didn't want to test just how sound-proof the back of this car was. His thumb rubbed over and around my clit until the pressure inside me exploded. I came with a muffled cry, my nails digging into Dax's arm until I knew I'd left marks.

I whimpered as he removed his hand from between my legs. What the hell had I gotten myself into?

My legs were still shaky when we pulled up in front of the hotel. Dax put his arm around my waist, holding me up as we checked in. The desk clerk didn't seem to know what to make of us. This wasn't the sort of place that rented by the hour, and I was pretty sure that it was clear why the two of us were here...without any luggage. There was also the fact of how out of place Dax looked in this fancy lobby. Even with his tattoos covered by his coat, there was something intimidating and maybe even a little scary about him.

Neither one of us said a word as we rode the elevator to the fourth floor, though we did both remove our coats. One less layer to take off once we got in the room. His hand was hot on my hip as we stepped out of the elevator, and every step we took down the hall made my body clench in anticipation. I hadn't let myself admit how much I wanted him until now, when it was impossible to deny.

The moment the door closed behind me, Dax pushed me

back against it and dropped to his knees. Before I could ask him what he was doing, he was tugging off my boots. Once those were free, he pushed my dress up around my waist and pulled off my panties. I stepped out of them, first using his shoulders for balance, then to hold myself up when his mouth pressed against me.

The strangled sound that came out as his tongue explored was a cross between his name and a moan. He'd used his fingers on me the first time, but not his mouth. I had friends who talked about having to convince their boyfriends to go down on them, and even then, they claimed it hadn't been very good.

Dax was good. Beyond good.

I ran a hand up his neck to grip his hair in my fist. His hands were on my hips, holding them in place as he found my clit. I cried out, a jolt of pleasure going through me. There was no teasing, no gentle easing into things. His tongue and lips were relentless, driving me towards another orgasm. His fingers dug into me with bruising force, but it wasn't too much. It was like he knew exactly where the line was between what I could handle and what I couldn't.

I remembered how Carrie and her friends had said that what most people didn't get about the whole BDSM lifestyle was how much trust was an essential part. Now, as I gave myself over to Dax, I understood what they meant. Only when I completely let go, when I trusted him not to take things too far, did I have the freedom to fully enjoy what he was doing.

I could only imagine what it would be like to trust him enough to venture into any other areas of S&M.

I called out his name as I came again, wave after wave of

white-hot pleasure washing over me, his mouth coaxing out every last bit until my knees buckled and he caught me in his arms.

By the time I came down from my high, I was on the bed, and he was standing next to it, naked. I took a moment to admire him. He'd kept his jeans on last time, but now I was able to follow the deep v-grooves at his hips, see the corded muscles in his thighs. Every tattoo and piercing, every inch of that gorgeous body.

I'd taken an art course my first semester in college, and we'd spent two weeks on the human form, complete with having to draw a nude based on the model posing for us. The teacher had dedicated an entire discussion to what was considered artistic perfection, and the point she'd made at the end was that people rarely agreed on what the ideal truly was.

I had a feeling that if Dax had been our model, pretty much all of the straight women and gay men would've agreed on him being a near-perfect male specimen.

"Strip, Bryne."

The hunger in his gaze made me shiver. I pulled my dress off, grateful that I'd picked something comfortable and easy to remove. The bra went next, and both ended up on the floor somewhere.

"I want you on your hands and knees." His voice rough, as if the words themselves were scraping his throat raw.

I rolled onto my stomach, then pushed myself up. A flush spread across my skin, first from embarrassment, then arousal as his hand ran over my ass and then up my back. My eyelids fluttered when his hand moved under me, covering one breast. His fingers teased me, pinching and rolling my nipple until I forgot all about being embarrassed and only thought about how perfect his touch was.

"You're so fucking beautiful."

I looked over my shoulder, my eyes meeting his. Every cell was throbbing, needing more than what he'd already given. I needed him inside me, and if the way his cock was twitching was any indication, he needed to be inside me as well. He kept his eyes on me as he rolled on a condom and then settled on his knees behind me.

A sharp smack on my ass made me jump, and I glared at him but didn't say a word when he did it again. The pain had been sharp, but quick, gone before it really registered. Now, all I felt was heat spreading out from where his hand had been. I'd never gotten the appeal of spanking before, but now I was starting to wonder if maybe I had more in common with Carrie and her friends than I thought.

The hand on my breast moved to my hair, wrapping it around his fist until he controlled the movement of my head. Still, I didn't protest. I may not have had much experience with actual sex, but I did know my own body, and what he was doing made me impossibly wet. My nipples were hard points, my hands digging into the comforter. I'd never been so turned on.

The tip of him brushed against me, and that was the only warning I received before he drove into me with one fast, hard thrust. The sound I made could only be described as a wail, a long, wordless cry, full of every sensation ripping through my body. Too many conflicting signals raced across my nerves, firing pain and pleasure receptors until my brain couldn't decide what I was feeling.

The muscles in my thighs quivered, and I wondered how long I'd be able to hold myself up as Dax began to move with slow, deliberate strokes. Each one went deep, filling me thoroughly before he withdrew almost all the way. There was no pause, no hesitation. He knew exactly what he was doing, exactly how to play my body.

I'd made a mistake, I realized, by having Dax be my first lover. I doubted any other man would be able to compare in bed. And I'd always compare them. I wouldn't be able to help it.

He tugged on my hair, using it as leverage while he rode my body, pushing us both toward the inevitable end. Every inch of me was overly sensitized from my two previous orgasms, my clit throbbing, my muscles clenching and squeezing. It wasn't going to take long.

His hand came down on my ass again, and that was all I needed. The sweet sting that made the heat in my belly boil over. This was a different orgasm than I'd ever had before, deeper somehow, and I closed my eyes to let it roll through and over me. I was dimly aware that I was calling out his name, but sound had little meaning at the moment. It was all about the place where our bodies joined, the places where we touched.

Then Dax gave a guttural groan, his body stiffening behind mine, and I knew he was coming. He pulled my hair hard enough to make my eyes water, his hand gripping my waist almost to the point of pain, and then his hands were gone, and my body was slumping down onto the bed.

I drifted as I heard him moving about a few moments later and wondered if he planned to pull a repeat of our first time. I hissed as a washcloth moved between my legs, the fabric rough against my sensitive skin, but I didn't push him away, and it wasn't only because I didn't have the strength. I wanted to see what he'd do next; if he'd actually wanted more than just a second round.

He moved me under the blankets and then crawled under with me. I could feel the uncertainty as he wrapped his arms around me, and I knew he was waiting to see if I would tell him to leave. I hadn't yet reached the level where words were possible again, so I snuggled closer to him instead and felt his body relax.

I didn't know what this meant, who we were to each other, or even if we'd both wake up and realize we'd made a mistake, but I wouldn't dwell on any of that now. Whatever the future held would come eventually, and we'd deal with it then. Tonight, I would let myself fall asleep in his arms, grateful that I'd come to New York.

Filled with hope for the wonderful things to come.

My phone ringing pulled me from a sweet, and dreamless sleep. As I rolled over and picked it up, I noticed two things in rapid succession. First, it was already nine thirty in the morning. Second, I had three missed calls, including the one that had just woken me up. Caller ID said the call came from a private number, which didn't really tell me much of anything, but whoever it was had at least left a voicemail so I could find out before I decided whether or not to call back.

It wasn't until I sat up to listen to the message that the deep throbbing ache between my legs reminded me I hadn't gone to bed alone. I glanced toward the empty space next to me, my stomach clenching as I realized Dax was gone.

Again.

Before I could read too much into it, however, my eye fell on a piece of paper that lay on the pillow beside me. The curtains were drawn so the room was still too dark for me to read the note, so I flipped on the light even as I unfolded the piece of paper.

Dinner tonight. Meet at the club.

Okay, so it wasn't a love note, or even an explanation as to where he'd gone, but it was something. More than something, actually. He could've just left a *thanks for a good time* and it would've been as good as last time. This was him saying that he wanted to see me again.

I shivered as I remembered the things he'd told me, the things he wanted to do to me. He'd done some of them, and I wondered if his note was a promise of more to come.

I wasn't going to assume any more than that. I'd entertained the idea of a friendship with him where sex was an option, and that was all I was going to hope for. We'd both said we didn't want a relationship, and I still meant it. I had too much else going on to deal with everything that came with dating. Especially dating someone like Dax. I didn't know a lot about him, but I knew enough to know that nothing would be simple.

Still, I couldn't stop the smile that came to my lips when I thought about being able to count on Dax for regular, mind-blowing sex. Maybe we could even get into some of the things he'd seen while working at Club Privé.

A part of me was tempted to text him, tell him to forget dinner, and come straight back to the hotel.

Instead, I did the responsible thing and picked up my phone to call my voicemail.

"Bryne, this is Jacqueline Jamison, the casting director for Collide. I'd like to send out your contract. I just have a couple questions. Give me a call."

I listened to the message twice to make sure I had the number right, and then called it back, all thoughts of Dax pushed aside. Well, most of them anyway. Considering how well-used my body felt, it'd be impossible for me not to have him hovering in the back of my mind for at least a couple days.

The conversation with Jacqueline was short, but when I ended the call, I felt like I'd taken a straight shot of caffeine or adrenaline or something. I was wide awake now, synapses humming. Jacqueline had a contract for me. What I'd come to New York for, what I'd been wanting to do since I was a kid, wasn't just a possibility anymore. It was actually happening.

And that meant I couldn't spend the rest of the morning lounging around in bed thinking about Dax and sex. I had things I had to do. The first of which was calling Carrie to tell her that I'd given her name as being the lawyer who'd look over my contract. I knew she wasn't an entertainment lawyer, but her friend Krissy worked in that field, and I knew Carrie would ask if she needed to.

The second thing I had to do was get in the shower because I wasn't about to leave the hotel looking like I'd just been well and truly fucked. Granted, I had, but I couldn't walk back into Carrie and Gavin's like that. Gavin was annoyed with me enough already as it was.

When I got out of the shower, however, I changed my plans. Todd had texted me. Apparently, he'd gotten his call today too, and wanted to meet for lunch to schedule practice times outside of general rehearsal. A thrill went through me as I read the message. Part of me was still waiting for someone to tell me that a mistake had been made, that things weren't really coming together for me so quickly.

Since Dax and I hadn't exactly planned our little liaison, I didn't have any clean clothes, but fortunately for me, the hotel had a boutique so I only had to go downstairs to find a cute sweater and skirt combination that would be perfect for lunch at Tavern on the Green.

The weather matched my mood as I stepped outside. Clear blue skies, bright shining sun. It was still cold, but it was the sort of cold I found invigorating. I had plenty of time before I was supposed to meet Todd, so rather than spending it in a cab, I opted for a walk to Central Park. The exercise would do me good. Work out all the kinks and stiff muscles that I'd accumulated thanks to dancing and sex.

Heat rushed to my cheeks, giving the cold air a bit more bite. I had a feeling Todd was going to want to know how things went with Dax last night, and if I was being completely honest, I wanted someone to talk to about it. Carrie wouldn't judge, I knew, but I didn't want to put her in an awkward position with Gavin. Better to keep them on a "need to know" basis when it came to any specifics with my sex life, especially when Dax was involved.

I was so caught up in thoughts of what could be in my future that I didn't notice someone walking straight toward me until she stopped directly in front of me. I pulled myself up short, just missing colliding with her.

"Sorry." I gave her a bright smile and moved to step around her.

Her hand shot out and grabbed my arm. I forced myself to keep the smile on my face. "Can I help you?"

Sunlight glinted off of the silver ring in her eyebrow as she glared at me. "Yeah, you can help me." She leaned close and I could smell the cigarette smoke on her breath. "Stay the fuck away from my man."

"Excuse me?" I racked my brain to try to find some recognition. Long light brown hair. Coal black eyes. Only a couple inches taller than me. Pretty in a rough kind of way. But I couldn't place her.

"Dax." Her fingers dug into my arm. "Stay away from him. He's mine."

She shoved me backwards and I barely kept myself from falling. She stalked past me without another word, leaving me to stare after her.

What the hell had just happened?

I'd gotten pretty good at lying, especially these last few years. My mom would've said I was a little too good if she'd known just how often I did it, but half the time, I did it to protect her. I tried not to lie too much to her face, but lying to myself was a different story. I told myself all sorts of shit so I'd do what needed to be done. I was pretty sure that wasn't one of my lies. It had only been me and Mom my whole life, and since she got hurt, it'd been my job to take care of her.

Okay, so maybe I used that as an excuse not to get involved with anyone, but the truth was, once I fucked a woman, I really didn't have any further use for her. I was sure some people considered me an asshole for having that attitude, but I always made sure the woman I was with knew that going in. I made sure she got off, and I never treated her like trash, which was more than some guys, but she knew the whole time it was only sex.

Bryne Dawkins hadn't been any different. She wasn't any different.

Dammit.

As I looked down at her, some small part of me called me out for lying. The lighting in the hotel room was dim, but I didn't need bright light to be able to see her perfectly. Her bronze curls were soft against my skin, and it was all I could do not to run my fingers through them. Her eyes were closed, but I knew their exact shade of green. They'd haunted me from the moment I first saw them, the day she walked into *DeMarco's & Sons.*

I told myself then that I just wanted to get hold of those soft curves, see what was hiding under those winter clothes. The moment I slid inside her though, I'd known once wouldn't be enough. I tried to deny it, tried to tell myself that she was out of my league. Hell, I'd known that from the second she walked into the shop, but it hadn't stopped me from wanting her. And getting her.

And she'd been nothing but trouble ever since.

Georgie, my buddy, had been pissed when I told him to back off, so when she turned up again, I'd behaved like an ass to drive her away. Then her aunt had fired me from Club Privé, which meant I lost the better half of my income. Confronting Bryne hadn't done anything but confirm what I'd been trying to deny for days.

I still wanted her.

My stomach clenched as she shifted in her sleep, her naked body rubbing against mine. Fuck. Even after having her again, I wanted nothing more than to bury my face between her legs until she woke up calling out my name, then see how many more times I could make her come on my cock.

Except that would be a bad idea, and no amount of lying to myself would change the truth of that.

Bryne wasn't naive, but she was definitely innocent. Hell, I could almost taste it on her. This city could chew up and spit out girls like her, and it would happen even faster if she was near me.

I forced myself from the bed, careful not to wake Bryne as I did. I wouldn't be able to leave if she woke up. One look from her, and I'd have a condom on and be inside her before either of us could think about why it was a bad idea.

Grabbing up my clothes, I crept out into the living room to dress. I should've left as soon as I wasn't bare-ass naked, but even as I took a step toward the door, I remembered what it had been like to walk out that first time, the way my heart had twisted at the expression on Bryne's face when I'd given her those flippant lines.

I couldn't do that to her again. No matter how many lies I told myself about what I wanted or didn't want, that was one thing I couldn't lie about. Hurting her hurt me.

And I knew if I ever wanted to see her again, I couldn't just go. I had to let her know I wasn't blowing her off.

My eyes had adjusted enough to the darkness that I was able to make my way over to the hotel desk. I found a piece of paper and pen easily enough. Before I could second guess myself, I jotted down a quick invitation to dinner and hoped she would take it.

I could've left the note anywhere, but I made myself walk back into the bedroom and put it on the side of the bed where I'd been sleeping so she wouldn't miss it. I didn't want her waking up and thinking I'd left her without a second thought. Hell, she was in all my thoughts pretty much all the time. I'd been a walking hard-on since I met her and fucking her hadn't helped. I was already half-hard by the time I got on the elevator.

I ignored the surprised look the desk clerk sent my way as I walked through the lobby. I didn't need some conde-scending prick to tell me I didn't look like I belonged there. A shiver went through me as I stepped outside, and I hunched my shoulders, trying to bury myself deeper in my coat. I hadn't paid much attention last night to where I was, so it took me a moment to catch my bearings before deciding that I could make it to the subway without freezing my ass off. I tried to avoid spending money on taxis, but sometimes it was just too damn cold to do it any other way.

I blew on my hands as I jogged down the steps, then fished my metro card out of my wallet. My mom insisted on me having one, and I used it often enough to keep her from suspecting how many times I hopped a turnstile rather than pay.

A pang of guilt went through me at the thought of my mom. I hadn't meant to fall asleep with Bryne, but the lack of sleep I'd had every night since meeting her was taking its toll. Add that into the fact that I'd basically been working two jobs non-stop for the last year, and it wasn't really surprising that I'd fallen asleep.

I doubted Mom would even be annoyed that I hadn't called. I'd be home before she woke up anyway. And she was always good about not pushing to know what I was out doing. She just wanted me to take care of myself.

I frowned as I took a seat. I was twenty-four years old. My mother didn't need to be thinking about how to take care of me, especially not after the year she'd gone through. She'd raised me all by herself, and I was the first to admit that I hadn't made it easy on her. I'd tried to stay away from the worst of things, despite how much pressure I'd gotten from Georgie and the guys to take part in the less-than-legal things that went on in the shop, but I couldn't say that I'd been a good kid. Not by a long-shot.

I sighed and ran my hand through my hair. Not for the first time, I wondered how different things would've been if my father had stuck around. Then again, for all I knew, things would've been worse. He could've been a complete asshole. Abusive. Alcoholic. A whole other list of things that was worse than absent.

I'd given up asking about him a long time ago. My birth certificate simply said *unknown*, but Mom always insisted she knew who he was. When I'd nagged her about it as a child, she'd only said that circumstances had prevented him from being a part of my life. Sometimes, I thought she meant that he died, but most of the time, I just figured he was married.

Or he simply hadn't wanted me.

I glowered at a punk teenager who tripped over my foot and swore at me. The kid flipped me off but hurried away before I could get up and teach him some respect.

I pushed myself to my feet as the first of my two changes came up. Mom and I lived in Hell's Kitchen, not too far from *DeMarco's & Sons*, and not too far from Club Privé either, but the hotel Bryne and I had gone to was on the opposite side of Manhattan. Still, I wouldn't complain. Sex with Bryne was worth every minute, and more. I didn't know how much experience she had, but she was definitely one of the best lays I'd ever had under me.

My stomach twisted with some unfamiliar sensation, and

it took me a moment to realize that it was jealousy. I didn't like thinking about how Bryne had gotten so good in bed.

Shit.

I needed to get myself under control. I couldn't be jealous because we weren't in a relationship. We could be friends. Maybe have sex when we felt like it. But nothing else. I couldn't do it.

Besides, she deserved better than me.

FIFTEEN

BRYNE

My head was spinning as I started making my way through Central Park again. It wasn't much farther to Tavern on the Green, or at least that's what my befuddled brain was trying to remember from the brief look I'd taken at the directions on my phone before I left the hotel.

When I woke up this morning to find Dax gone, I feared I'd made a horrible mistake by sleeping with him again. Then I'd seen his note asking me to meet him for dinner. Well, *asking* might not have been the right word. It was more like a strong suggestion. I hadn't known Dax long, but I'd already gotten the impression that he didn't do much in the way of making requests.

But it wasn't Dax I was thinking about as I hurried toward the restaurant. Not him directly anyway. He'd been on my mind when I first set off, but that had changed a few minutes ago when a strange woman approached me. And strange wasn't only because I'd never seen her before. Probably only a couple years older than me, she had multiple piercings and the angriest expression I'd seen in a long time.

Her appearance wasn't what had me freaking out though. No, it was because she'd told me, in no uncertain terms, to stay away from Dax.

I'd been in New York City for about a week, and I'd already snuck into a sex club, lost my virginity, got the lead in my first off-Broadway play, and been threatened over a guy.

I wasn't entirely sure I wanted to know what came next.

When I stepped into Tavern on the Green, Todd Emery was already waiting. Strawberry blond hair, smokey gray eyes, and absolutely gorgeous, he had almost every woman in the restaurant looking at him. A good portion of men were too. The best thing about him, however, was that he had a perfect balance of confidence and humility. He knew he was attractive but didn't let it go to his head.

He frowned as he looked at me, then opened his arms. I stepped into them without hesitating. Todd was the romantic lead opposite me in the play *Collide*, but I didn't have to worry about him taking any of this the wrong way. He was completely committed to his boyfriend, Hiram, which allowed me to accept the comfort without any awkwardness attached.

After a moment, I stepped back. Todd let me go, but his hand settled on the small of my back as he led the way to a table near the back. He waited until I took off my coat, and we both were settled into our seats before speaking.

"Are you okay?"

I let out a shaky laugh. "Honestly, I'm not entirely sure."

I quickly filled him in on everything that had happened since I'd last seen him, which, strangely enough, had only

been last night. I'd been with him at Club Privé before Dax
had shown up. It felt like it'd been years though. When I
finished, silence fell for several long seconds before he let out
a breath.

"Wow. That's...a lot."

"Tell me about it," I muttered.

We paused in our discussion to place our orders, and I
wondered if Todd was going to move off to another subject
when we were done. Most of the kids I'd spent time around
growing up would've shown interest for a moment, then tried
to make it about them. I didn't have a problem giving a
listening ear or offering advice to someone else, but my brain
was so scrambled at the moment, I wasn't sure I could
manage any genuine concern or interest in anything else.
Especially since I didn't know what the hell I was going to do
about the warning I'd received.

Not for the first time, however, Todd surprised me. One
of the ways my mother had tried to discourage me from
moving to New York had been to tell me that the people in
the Big Apple were rude...and then added a few other less-
than-complimentary descriptions. Todd had completely
disproved all of that. Granted, there was a good chance he
was the exception rather than the rule, but since he was my
closest non-relative friend, I was happy enough with it.

"So, what do you want to do?" he asked.

"*Do?*" I echoed the word like I'd never heard it before.
"About the hot guy I had sex with, or the scary chick who told
me to stay away from him?"

"Seems to me that they're pretty linked," he said. "Question is, are you more scared of the woman who threatened
you, or do you like him enough not to care?"

I sighed and leaned back in my seat. "I'm not supposed to like him."

"Who says?" Todd grabbed a fry from my plate before the waiter could even set it down.

"Him." I breathed out a long exhale. "And me too, I guess."

"Elaborate."

I took a bite of the wild mushroom risotto, and then quickly explained the whole "no relationship" conversation during mine and Dax's original encounter. While Dax had said he still wanted me, and he apparently wanted to meet for dinner tonight, neither one of us had brought up whether or not this changed things.

"Do you want things to change?" Todd asked.

I thought about the way Dax kissed me, fierce and possessive, like he was claiming me. How his hands felt on my body. The way we moved together. Physically, my body responded to him, there was no doubt about that whatsoever. But did I want something more?

"I don't know," I answered honestly. "So much in my life has changed in the past couple weeks. I don't know if adding a relationship on top of everything else is a good idea."

He smothered his salad with pepper. "That's one way to look at it."

"What's another way?" I asked.

His expression grew thoughtful, and he turned his attention to his food. I didn't interrupt though. He'd answer me when he decided how he wanted to say it. Until then, I'd enjoy the rest of my risotto. The silence between us was comfortable, more so than I'd ever experienced with anyone else.

"Back in DC, what were your relationships like?" Half of his Cobb salad was gone by the time he spoke.

I stared down at my food and hoped the blush I could feel creeping up my cheeks wasn't as obvious as it felt. "I didn't really have any."

"Are you kidding me?" The surprise in his voice showed on his face. "Were all the guys you knew gay or blind? I mean, hell, I'm gay and I'm pretty sure I'd have asked you out in high school."

I shook my head, eyes narrowing as I glared at him. "Pretty much every guy I came into contact with in DC were entitled assholes."

Curiosity flashed across Todd's face. "You never mentioned what your parents do."

"Before he died, my dad was a boxer." I hedged my answer. "My mom did some part-time work."

"Doesn't sound like you traveled in the circles of 'entitled assholes.'"

I had a feeling that if I didn't tell him what he wanted to know, he'd keep at me until I finally did. At least I was pretty sure he wouldn't treat me weird once he found out.

"My mom's family has money," I said finally. "Plus, Nana and Papa had been active in politics for years, so when Mom and I moved in with them, we got involved too."

"They were your grandparents?"

I shook my head. "My great-grandparents, actually. Remember how I told you about how Gavin and my mom have the same father? Well, the whole thing caused a huge rift between my grandmother and her parents."

Todd looked like he wanted to ask more, but turned the subject back to me and Dax. "So all the guys you were around in DC were jerks, which meant you didn't have a serious boyfriend?"

I could see the other question coming, so I answered it before he could ask. "Dax was my first."

Todd let out a low whistle.

"It's not a big deal," I snapped and stabbed a piece of broccoli with my folk.

He grinned and raised an eyebrow. "It wasn't...*big*?"

"Bite me."

He laughed, then sobered as he asked, "Does Dax know?"

"No." I pointed my fork at my friend. "And that's neither here nor there?"

"Okay, I might not be the best expert in female virginity, Bryne, but if you waited until you were nineteen to have sex, I don't think you can write-off feeling more than the warm fuzzies for the guy you finally gave it to."

"First," I emphasized the word by stealing a forkful of Todd's salad. "I never said I had warm fuzzies for Dax. And second, you're definitely not an expert in female virginity, so butt out."

In what I was learning was true Todd fashion, he gave me a little smirk. "I think I hit a nerve."

"Fine, Todd," I said with a huff of air that wasn't Four Season etiquette. "If you're so smart, what do you think I should do about Dax and my mystery threatener?"

The pleased look on his face told me that I'd asked exactly what he wanted. "Follow your heart."

I waited to hear the rest, but when several seconds passed without him saying anything else, I realized he was done.

"Are you shitting me?" He laughed, ignoring the fact that

I was giving him my best glower. "Seriously, Todd. Is that really it? *Follow my heart?*"

He shrugged. "What can I say? I'm a romantic."

"Yeah, well, I've seen what happens when people follow their traitorous, easily deceived heart."

"They get to be with the person they love?"

I set my fork down. I wasn't hungry anymore. "They get their hearts ripped out and stomped on by size thirteens."

My chest tightened as I thought of the women I knew who'd followed their hearts, who'd gone after the men they loved. My grandmother had loved Chauncey Manning, but he'd walked away from her and my mother. My parents had gotten married when my mom had gotten pregnant, but they loved each other, and my father had been there for me up until his death. He hadn't chosen to leave us, but his absence still hurt my mom, even after all these years.

Todd's hand closed over mine. "Hon, take it from me. If you don't at least see what this might be with Dax, you'll regret it. Maybe nothing will come of it. And, yeah, maybe your heart gets broken, but isn't that better than not knowing?"

Silence fell again, but this time, I was in no rush to break it. Todd had given me a lot to think about before I met Dax tonight.

SIXTEEN

I wasn't a monk, but until today, I'd never gotten dressed for a date. Even when I had casual flings where I'd been with a girl for more than one or two nights, I didn't really date. Hell, I could count on one hand the number of women I'd taken to get something to eat. Most of the time, I either found someone at work or had them meet me there, then we'd go back to her place and fuck.

I didn't take anyone home with me.

The types of girls I had sex with weren't anyone I wanted near my mother. They were generally loud, both in personality and appearance. Trashy clothes. Tattoos. And almost all of them had piercings, generally in some pretty sensitive places. I'd had more blow jobs from girls with tongue studs than without.

Most were chicks who came into the shop, looking to be fucked by someone like me. Every so often, I'd find someone at Club Privé who was more interested in the help than the patrons, but even then it was never one of the classy members. It was usually someone who'd managed to wrangle a visit, thinking they wanted something the club had to offer. Some of them came back to the club once or twice, but that was always with some important member who probably wouldn't have wanted to know that they were getting my sloppy seconds.

I frowned at my reflection, but I wasn't sure if I was frowning because I knew my mother would've beaten my ass if she'd known how I was with women. She'd taught me how to treat women, and I'd always been respectful to her. I'd just never met another woman I felt deserved to be treated that well. Okay, Carrie Manning did. She was a good person, and her friends were decent too. If a woman my age who was like them ever wanted to be with me, she would be someone I could introduce to my mom.

Thing was, as I looked at the stranger in the mirror, I had a feeling that Bryne was the sort of woman Mom would actually like. She was down-to-earth and knew what she wanted. Didn't take shit from anyone, including me, and she was smart, respected herself. She looked good but didn't act like it made her better than anyone else.

I couldn't say that I'd never met anyone like her before, because I had. I'd just never had someone like her give me a second look.

I took a slow breath and reminded myself that she hadn't just given me a second look. She'd gone to bed with me. Twice. And unless I was wrong about what happened between us last night, she'd meet me at the club tonight. Once might've been slumming it. Twice, not so much. If she showed up at Club Privé, it would mean that fucking me wasn't just something she'd decided to try out.

When I came into the living room, I was surprised to see my mom sitting on the couch rather than already being in her room like she usually was by this time. The injuries she'd gotten at work were healed, but she'd be doing rehab and getting her strength back for at least another six months. She hated how tired she felt all the time, but I kept telling her that she needed to take it slow. She was my only family, and I'd come too close to losing her. I wouldn't let that happen again.

I pushed those thoughts out of my head as I smiled at her. "You need anything before I go?"

We looked a lot alike, Mom and me. Same dark hair color that she insisted was cocoa brown. Her eyes were darker blue while mine, she contended, were cobalt. But we shared enough of the same features that I wondered if I had any of my dad in me at all.

"You look awfully dressed up for work."

She looked tired, but she didn't miss anything.

"New jeans."

The look she gave me told me that she knew I was deflecting. "You didn't come home last night."

"I did." I opted for a half-truth. "You were asleep already."

Again, that knowing look.

"I have to go, Mom." I leaned down and kissed the top of her head. "Don't tire yourself out too much."

"You either."

I could hear the smile and knew that I'd never be able to fool her. She'd always known me so well. I closed the door behind me, locked both it and the deadbolt. We didn't live in the worst neighborhood, but it wasn't the best either.

I took the subway to Club Privé and wondered if Bryne

would be there when I arrived. My fingers drummed on my knee as I waited for my stop. Nervous energy raced through me. I'd never felt anything like it.

Actually, that wasn't exactly true, I realized. The first time I'd seen Bryne, I felt a similar excitement. Every time I was with her, I felt like I was holding a live wire. Something about her made me feel more alive than I'd ever felt.

It was dangerous, what I was doing. Dangerous for me...and for Bryne.

My hand curled into a fist at the thought of anyone hurting Bryne, and I got to my feet, unable to stay seated. I couldn't think that way, think of all the ways this could go sideways. Hell, I didn't even know what *this* was, and I didn't want to take too much on when, for all I knew, Bryne could've decided that I wasn't worth it.

If I'd been in her position, I would've written me off.

I had to take it one step at a time, keep reminding myself that I could still live in the moment without planning how I would keep her from getting too attached. I didn't want to even think about making sure I wasn't the one getting attached. It couldn't happen. I wouldn't let it.

The war inside me continued all the way to the club, making me second-guess my decision to do this whole dinner thing. As the front of Club Privé came into view, I almost turned around and walked away, almost convinced myself that it would be better for both of us if I stood her up and left things broken between us.

And then I saw those wild curls, and that short, curvy body, and I knew I couldn't walk away. Not yet anyway. I had to get inside her again.

"You got my note." I mentally kicked myself for not coming up with a better greeting.

"I did." She smiled up at me and linked her arm through mine. "So, where are we going to eat?"

"What are you in the mood for?" Even as I asked the question, I hoped that she wouldn't name some pricey five-star restaurant. The few women I'd taken to dinner had been fine with me picking a fairly inexpensive place, mostly because they'd assumed I'd find someone else if they complained. They were right.

Bryne was different.

"Anywhere that's not outside is fine with me." She flashed another smile. "Though I'd prefer no fast food."

"I think I can manage that." I held out a hand to hail a taxi. No way was I going to have her riding the subway.

I gave the driver an address as I slid inside, then wrapped my arm around Bryne when she settled next to me. It surprised me how natural the gesture felt, more like she belonged there rather than I was pulling her in to try to cop a feel. As we rode in silence, dozens of questions kept creeping up in my brain, most of them about why I was taking Bryne to my mother's favorite restaurant. I'd never taken anyone there before, and a part of me warned that I was taking this thing with Bryne too far.

When I saw the delight on her face when she walked inside the little family-owned restaurant, my doubts retreated. The entire place was strung with clear Christmas lights, sending unique shadows playing against the old brick walls. A handful of people were seated around the dining room, and a few glanced our way as a familiar middle-aged redhead approached.

"Dax!" Addison beamed at me. "It's been too long! How's your mom?"

"Better." I put my hand on the small of Bryne's back and wished she wasn't wearing a winter coat. I didn't like the extra layers between us. "Addison, this is Bryne. Bryne, Addison here owns the place."

"It's beautiful," Bryne said sincerely as she held out her hand.

"Thank you." Addison picked up two menus and gestured for us to follow her. "My grandfather started it when he was twenty, and it's been in my family ever since."

Bryne shrugged off her coat, revealing an off-the-shoulder fitted sweater to go with her form-hugging jeans. I gave her a heated look as she sat down, and a faint blush stained her cheeks. The fact that she blushed instead of acting like she deserved the attention made me wonder how stupid the other men she'd dated had been.

Not that we were dating.

"You and your mom come here?" she asked.

I nodded. "She and Addison went to school together, and we'd come by every few weeks."

She opened the menu. "Then you should know what's best to eat."

As I started to go through my favorites, I realized how much I wanted her to like it here. Despite my resolve to keep things in the friendship zone – hopefully with benefits – I couldn't seem to stop myself from wanting more. I knew I'd have to deal with it sooner or later, but I wasn't going to do it now. Right now, I planned to enjoy a meal with a beautiful woman.

I WISHED Bryne and I could've gone to Club Privé, even if only to dance, but I'd used up the little bit of extra cash I had on dinner, and I wasn't about to let Bryne know that I couldn't afford a cover charge or drinks. That meant our choices were limited, so I just said we were going to a club that was closer. A friend of mine was the doorman there, so we wouldn't have to wait in line.

"You have a lot of friends," she commented as we started to walk.

I shrugged. *Friend* might've been too strong a word for most of the people I knew. Addison was one, but there were very few others. More like acquaintances with mutual interests. This particular one was Georgie's cousin, but I wouldn't tell Bryne that. She hadn't really said much about the guys from the shop, but I didn't need her to say a word to know that she definitely didn't like Georgie.

The music was blaring so loud that we could hear the bass before the door even opened, but I didn't mind. We'd talked over dinner. Now, I wanted to get physical. I tossed our coats towards another of Georgie's cousins, then grabbed Bryne's hand and pulled her toward the dance floor.

I put one hand on her hip, and we started to move. We found the rhythm easily enough, and she didn't protest when I moved closer. There were bodies all around us, brushing against us as we danced, but hers was the only one I was aware of. Aware didn't even seem to be a strong enough word, but it was the only one I could think of that got even close.

Her breasts brushed against me, and my erection pressed painfully against my zipper. Out of necessity – I hadn't done laundry in almost two weeks – I was going commando tonight, but now I was starting to think that had been a bad idea.

She turned around, pulling my arm with her so that my hand rested on her hipbone. Air hissed from between my teeth as she pushed her ass back against my crotch. The look she threw over her shoulder told me that she knew exactly what she was doing to me. My fingers dug into her, and I wished she'd worn a dress tonight. I would've made her regret teasing me.

I clenched my jaw as new images assaulted me. Sliding my hand up her bare leg, moving under her skirt, and then over her panties. Cupping her over soft fabric and feeling how wet she was for me. Slipping my hand beneath the waistband, fingers skimming through curls before dipping between dripping folds.

The thought of fingering her to climax right here on the dance floor was too much. I needed to see her come.

Now.

I grabbed her wrist and pulled her after me. I'd never worked here, but I'd been here often enough that no one thought twice about me pushing open the door that said "Employees Only" like I owned the place. The hallway was dimly lit, the red exit sign glowing from the end, but I wasn't going that far. The first door on the right led to the basement where the alcohol was kept. The second was the manager's office. The only door on the left, however, was a janitor's closet. Not exactly romantic, but I didn't care.

I turned on the light, did a quick sweep of the small space, then reached over Bryne to shut the door. Her body pressed against me as I took her mouth. Her tongue slid across mine without any hesitation, her nails lightly scratching the back of my neck. I grabbed her ass with one hand, the other fisting her hair. I maneuvered her until the back of her boots bumped against the wooden pallet I'd seen.

I tore my mouth away, her sound of protest sending heat coursing through me. I spun her around and ordered, "Up."

A look of confusion flitted across her face, followed quickly by understanding. Even with heeled boots, she was still a lot shorter than me. The quickest way for this to happen was from behind, and for that, she needed to be standing on something.

I dug a condom out of my wallet and freed my dick. Even as I put the rubber on, Bryne was pushing her jeans and underwear down her thighs. I muttered a curse under my breath as she bared her ass. I usually prided myself on my staying power, but I wasn't going to last long. Not with her leaning forward, wiggling her hips in a blatant invitation.

I moved behind her and ran my hand between her legs. A shiver went through her, and my fingers came away wet. Everything in me was screaming to just slam into her, but I remembered how tight she was, and knew that without fore-play, I'd hurt her.

That didn't mean I had to be gentle.

I pushed two fingers inside her, my cock twitching as she made a strangled sound. I pumped them in quick, twisting strokes, stretching her as much as I could with the limited space and time we had.

I leaned down to bite her earlobe before saying, "This is the perfect position to fuck your ass." Her muscles clenched around my fingers. "Have you ever had a cock there?"

She shook her head, and my stomach tightened at the

thought of getting to take that cherry. Not right now though. I'd want her to enjoy it, and that meant preparation. She wasn't like other girls I'd been with who would take me with little more than some lube and a word.

"We'll put that on the to-do list." I pulled my fingers out of her pussy and reached around her. She didn't even wait for me to tell her to clean them, her tongue darting out to get two licks in before I slid them into her mouth.

The head of my cock brushed against her, and as I moved my hand from her mouth to her hair, she pushed her ass back toward me. She let out a soft cry as I drove into her, filling her with one thrust. Her pussy was almost painfully tight, but I didn't wait. Hell, I wasn't sure I could. I wrapped one arm around her waist and kept the other in her hair, holding her in place as I started to move.

My strokes were short, each one going as deep as I could, wanting to reach every last inch until I owned her body. I wanted to make sure I banished every other partner from her mind, that mine was the only touch she wanted. I wanted to ruin her for other men. I was already half sure that she'd ruined me.

I yanked her back by her hair, earning another of those hot little yelps she'd been making. I pulled her head to the side and pressed my mouth against the place where her shoulder and neck met. The pressure building inside me was intense, and I knew I was close. I just needed to get her there first. As I dropped the hand on her waist down between her legs, I sucked on her skin hard enough to leave a mark. She cried out my name when I bit down, then swore when my fingers found her clit.

I'd barely begun to rub her before she came unglued. Her

body stiffened, every muscle tensing as she came. I pushed myself hard inside her, my fingers still moving over her swollen clit until she came again. She shuddered, and the sensation of her muscles rippling around my cock pushed me over the edge.

We stood there for a minute as we came down, our bodies still joined, the only sound in the room our ragged breathing. I couldn't look away from the mark I'd left on her neck, unable to tell myself that I'd gotten carried away. Even if I hadn't admitted it to myself at the time, I knew that a deep and primal part of me had wanted to mark her, to let everyone else know that she was mine.

I closed my eyes even as my arm tightened around her waist. What was this woman doing to me?

SEVENTEEN

BRYNE

New York City had something in the water that turned me into someone completely different than I'd been in DC. That had to be it. After all, it was the only reasonable explanation for why I was pulling up my pants after having had sex in a janitor's closet. Sex with the man who'd taken my virginity when he'd been little more than a stranger. A dangerous-looking stranger with tattoos all over his arms and torso. And I couldn't forget his nipple piercing. Not when I still wanted to see what would happen if I used my tongue to play with it.

Fuck. I wanted him again.

"Ready?"

I looked over at Dax, who was holding out a hand to me, his expression impassive. I took his hand but didn't say anything as we walked back out into the club. I wasn't going to over think this, whatever *this* was. I'd simply accept the fact that my entire body was still tingling from an almost brutal orgasm.

I hadn't read a whole lot in the romance department, but in one book, I remembered reading a sentence that used the phrase "wrung an orgasm out of her." I understood that wording now. Dax hadn't hurt me, but he definitely hadn't been gentle either.

Growing up, dating and sex hadn't ever been priorities, but on the occasions where I thought about it, fantasized about it, it was always passionate, but nothing like what I'd experienced with Dax.

The thing that worried me as Dax pulled me against his side was something I hadn't taken into consideration. While some people always compared kisses to a first perfect kiss, most people didn't tend to do that with their first sexual experience. From everything I'd heard, most of the time, it was awkward and often disappointing. The fact that my first time had been the kind of sensual experience that should've only existed in the pages of some steamy romance novel, and each time after that had been just as good, made me worry that I was setting myself up for disappointment.

My body pulsed in time with the beat of the music, and even though I knew I was going to be sore tomorrow – I was already starting to feel it – I wanted more. I wanted to dance with him, feel his body pressed against mine. It wasn't just about getting us worked up either. I wanted to show every woman in here that I'd had him, and I would be having him again.

The spot on my neck where he'd bit me didn't hurt, but I was definitely aware of its presence. I didn't know if he meant anything by it, or if it was a heat of the moment kind of thing, but I couldn't stop myself from hoping he wanted people to see it, and know that we were together.

Well, not *together* together, because he wasn't my boyfriend. We weren't dating. A date had to be labeled as a date and agreed upon, right? And we definitely hadn't done that. We talked at dinner, but we never broached the subject of what it was. Which meant we weren't on a date.

As we made our way around the dance floor, Dax stiffened next to me. I looked up but wasn't surprised to see that I couldn't read a single thing on his face. I followed the direction of his gaze, hoping for a clue to what was going on...and my own body tensed.

Coming straight toward Dax and me was a familiar, and unwelcome, figure. Long light brown hair, eyes as black as coal. Enough metal on her face to make me wonder what happened when she went somewhere with a metal detector. She shot me a glare, but for the most part, her gaze was fixed on Dax.

He started to walk past her when she reached out and grabbed his arm. He looked down at her hand, up at her, then raised an eyebrow.

"Outside." She had to shout to be heard.

Dax gave a sharp nod and led the way, practically dragging me behind him. As we went, I wasn't entirely sure I wanted to hear this conversation. Clearly, Dax knew who she was. I'd assumed as much, but there was a difference between assuming and knowing.

I shivered as soon as we stepped outside, remembering that Dax had handed our coats to someone when we first arrived. His arm went around me, and he pulled me against his side. The embrace felt stiff, but I wasn't going to complain. He was warm.

"What do you want, Cleo?" Dax's voice was flat, almost bored-sounding.

"Haven't seen you in a while." She gave him the sort of smile that told me exactly what she meant by *seen*.

"What do you want?" he repeated. "As you can see, I'm busy."

Busy. Yeah, that was one way to describe it.

"We have a..." one side of her mouth lifted in a smirk, "*mutual friend* who wants to talk to you."

I worked to keep a frown off my face. I didn't like the sound of that, but I didn't want either Dax or Cleo to know. Dax wasn't mine. Not in the sense that I had the right to know things about him, or to feel anything about his life. We weren't even close enough as friends for me to ask about what was going on.

Still, I wasn't prepared for what Dax did next.

"Do you have a car you can call?"

It took me a moment to realize that he was talking to me. I nodded, repressing a shiver as he dropped his arm and took a step away from me.

"A security guy is standing just inside the door," Dax said, his eyes not meeting mine. "Tell him you need your coat, and stay inside until your car gets here. You don't need to be out here alone."

I wanted to snap back that if he cared that much, he could damn well stay with me, but I didn't. We weren't like that. And if I had to tell myself that over and over until it got through, I would.

I turned and walked back toward the door without responding. I wasn't sure I could keep my temper if I opened my mouth. Especially with the daggers Cleo was shooting at me. I doubted I would've liked her even if she hadn't threatened me.

I found the guy Dax mentioned, and while he was getting my coat, I pulled out my phone and called up the town car my uncle had reserved for family. Unlike some other car services, Gavin's was open twenty-four seven, so I knew I wouldn't have to wait long for someone to come for me.

When I was at Club Privé, I knew I was out of place, but I'd also known the reason – I was underage. Well, that and the obvious fact that it was a sex club. Here, I knew I was technically too young, but that wasn't why I felt awkward standing near the exit by myself. When Dax and I first arrived here, I'd seen that this place wasn't as nice as Club Privé, but I hadn't *felt* it until now. There was a definite difference between the people I'd been around at my uncle's club and the ones here. Some people might've thought it was about the money since Club Privé was private, elite, but I'd been around money long enough to know that wasn't it. I'd felt safe at my uncle's club, even before I knew he owned it. Here, I wasn't about to let down my guard.

That meant it wasn't until I was in the back of one of Gavin's cars, on my way back home, that all those thoughts about Dax started pushing forward. I still felt more like a guest at Carrie and Gavin's loft, but New York was starting to feel more like home than DC ever had. I'd loved Nana and Papa, and I'd always known they loved me. They never made me feel like I owed them anything.

But it hadn't been home.

Especially once I told my mother that I was moving to

New York. Things had been pretty tense around the house after that. We'd exchanged a couple texts since I arrived in the city, but no way could I go to her to talk over what happened tonight.

The problem was, I didn't think I could talk to Carrie either. The last time I'd discussed Dax with my aunt, she'd fired him from his security job at Club Privé. I didn't want to think what she'd do if I told her about Cleo warning me away from him, or the fact that Dax had pretty much blown me off with one word from her.

I kept telling myself that he hadn't been happy to see Cleo, and he certainly hadn't been flirting. His sending me home had to do with whoever this "mutual friend" of theirs was and not anything to do with me.

That didn't keep my mind from trying to show me images of Dax and Cleo together. Of him taking her to the same back room we'd been in and peeling off her painted-on leather pants so he could fuck her. Of her moaning his name. Him saying hers. Marking her like he'd marked me.

"Knock it off," I muttered to myself.

I wasn't the jealous type, at least I didn't think I was, although I'd never been in a relationship long enough to really know. Besides, Dax didn't seem to like Cleo very much. Surely he wouldn't have sex with someone he didn't like when he'd just had sex with someone he did. Because I was certain he like me. As a friend, of course. Nothing more.

And that was the other thing I needed to keep remembering. I had no claim on Dax, and he had none on me. We were friends, or at least well on our way there. Even if we kept the "with benefits" part of things, it wasn't a relationship.

After I thanked my driver and headed inside, I realized

that the fidgeting I'd been doing in the car hadn't been as absent-minded as I thought.

My fingers kept tracing around and over the dark mark Dax's mouth had left on my skin.

I sighed. Dammit. This wasn't part of my plan.

EIGHTEEN

DAX

I told myself that the reason I hated watching Bryne go back into the club without me was because I'd been looking forward to fucking her again. Having her only a few minutes ago wasn't even close to enough. Hell, I'd just come, and was already half-hard from thinking about being inside that tight pussy again.

My desire for sex couldn't completely rationalize the fact that I'd told her to stay inside until her car came. I wasn't a total asshole who didn't care about women being safe, but with anyone else, I doubted the thought would've crossed my mind. I would've assumed she knew how to take care of herself and left it at that. I knew Bryne was capable, but the thought of something happening to her had me wanting to go after her so I could make sure she was safe.

I had to keep my cool though. It wouldn't be smart to let anyone know the sorts of thoughts Bryne made me have. Especially not Cleo.

As I looked down at her, she pulled a pack of cigarettes

from her pocket and lit one up. She held the pack out to me, and I shook my head, glaring at her. The only grandparent I remembered had died from lung cancer when I was a kid. Remembering how Gramp had looked those last couple months had always been enough to keep me from lighting a death stick.

And Cleo damn well knew it.

We'd gone out on and off for a few months a couple of years ago, and while I'd never gone so far as to call her my girlfriend, she knew more about me than anyone else I'd been with. I didn't even like to say that we dated because that implied something even less casual than what we'd had. We'd hung out a decent amount, but it wasn't because I'd asked her to or anything. One of her cousins worked at the shop, and she'd always made that her excuse.

I'd practically been fucking her by default. I'd never led her on, but that wasn't how she saw it.

"Now that you've lost the excess baggage, how about you and me have a little fun before we go?" She ran one long fingernail down my arm.

"Not interested." I stuck my hands in my pockets. "Tell me what you're doing here."

A scowl twisted her lips, and she crossed her arms. Some people might've thought she was standing that way because she was angry, but I knew she was trying to get me to look at her breasts. Why else would she have her coat unzipped in the middle of January?

"Like I said, we have–"

I cut her off. "Who is it? And you better not have made it up."

"Booker."

Shit.

I'd suspected that was whom she meant when she hadn't said his name, but I'd still been hoping this was all some sort of game she was playing.

"Where is he?"

"Follow me."

I wanted to grab her and make her tell me where we were going, but it didn't really matter. If Booker North wanted to see me, and he'd sent Cleo to get me, then I had to assume that he wanted her to escort me to him. If he'd told her to just to give me the location, and she was being ignorant, it was his problem, not mine. And Cleo knew better than to piss Booker off, which meant she was most likely following exactly what he'd told her to do.

Booker was in his mid-thirties and was one of the scariest sons of bitches I'd ever come across. Georgie liked to run his mouth and talk big, but he didn't do shit without Booker's permission. Booker not only owned *DeMarco's & Sons*, but he was the one to kill old man DeMarco and the two sons.

At least, that was the rumor. No one really knew what actually happened to them. Less than two days after the old man refused to sell Booker the shop, the family disappeared, and Booker was the new owner. Case closed. No one spoke of it again.

Georgie was the one who'd gotten me a job at the shop when I was sixteen, and I'd suspected that many of the other guys there were in the same gang as him. Since I'd never been a member, I hadn't realized that someone new had taken over a few years ago until I showed up at work to find the DeMarco's gone. There'd been a change in leadership, and now Georgie was number two to the new leader. They'd pretty much left me alone since I kept my mouth shut, but I'd always been aware that, someday, that would probably change.

I'd met Booker only once, and it wasn't an experience I was eager to repeat, but knowing that he'd asked to see me and that he'd sent Cleo instead of Georgie, was a good indication that this wouldn't lead anywhere good.

I knew the gang did a lot of unsavory shit, but the shop was only involved in selling stolen car and motorcycle parts. Well, that and some money laundering. I had no doubt that some of the guys I worked with had decent rap sheets and probably violent offenses, but none of them measured up against what Booker was rumored to be into.

By the time we got to the subway, I was trying not to shiver and was mentally cursing Cleo for not telling me I'd need my coat. When we got off near the shop, I was pissed as well as cold. If she'd just told me that we were coming here, I could've gotten my coat and followed her.

I didn't say anything though. I might not have gotten the best grades in school, but I was no idiot. I knew when it was time to keep my mouth shut and my eyes open, and this was definitely one of those times.

We went inside, Cleo still leading the way. When we passed the break room, she spoke, "Remember how many times we fucked in there? It used to turn me on, knowing the guys were out here, listening."

I remembered. I also remembered how she'd leave the door unlocked and talk about how she hoped Georgie or someone would come in and ask to join us even after I told her I wasn't into threesomes, especially not with another guy.

Yet another reason why I didn't feel guilty for breaking

things off with her. She liked to act like the two of us had been in some serious relationship, but I knew she was fucking other guys at the same time, trying to make me jealous. When she'd thrown a tire iron at one of my one-night stands a year ago, that had been the last straw. I told her I didn't want to see her at all.

Since she'd gone to jail for assault a week later, that hadn't been an issue, but I'd heard she'd gotten out a couple weeks ago and wondered if she'd come back around. I hadn't figured she'd be playing messenger for Booker though.

We stopped at the office, and she knocked.

"Come in." Booker's gravelly voice came from the other side of the door.

She pushed open the door and smirked at me before walking away. Apparently, she wasn't part of this conversation, which meant that Booker had either sent her to piss me off, or she'd volunteered for the same reason. Either way, I was on edge when I walked into the office and saw Booker leaning against the shitty metal desk.

Almost six and a half feet tall, bald, and with more tattoos showing than I had on my entire body, he was the type of person people were scared they'd run into in New York. And he didn't just look scary. He backed it up.

"Dax."

"Booker." I kept my expression neutral, knowing that Booker didn't respect ass-kissers, but he would also beat the shit out of anyone he thought was being disrespectful. It wasn't a fun line to walk.

"Sit." He jerked his chin toward the only chair in the room.

I didn't want to sit, especially since I had no idea why

Booker wanted to talk to me, but I wasn't stupid enough to disobey. I made myself look comfortable, but every muscle was tense. I didn't pay much attention in school, but one of the things from biology that I'd always remembered had been the whole fight or flight response, and I felt it now. Adrenaline coursed through me, and it took every ounce of self-control I had to keep myself from moving. Fighting or running, I didn't know which, but I did know that I didn't want to be doing nothing.

"Georgie tells me you do good work," Booker began. "And he says you know how to keep your mouth shut."

I gave a short nod, my fingers drumming against my thigh.

"He also says you know some of the other stuff that goes on here."

"I do." The words came out even despite the knots working through my stomach.

"But you've never asked to get in on a job." He made it a statement rather than a question, then went on without waiting for me to acknowledge it. "And as long as it didn't cause problems, I told Georgie to let you do your own thing."

I almost frowned as I tried to figure out what I possibly could've done that was causing problems, but I managed to keep my face blank and waited to hear what Booker had to say next.

"I'm expanding my business," he continued. "And that means you'll be stepping up."

I didn't like the sound of that, especially since it didn't seem like he was asking.

"I've got a job planned, and we're one man short." He pointed a finger at me. "You're that man."

Fuck my life.

Two damn days.

Two silent, aggravating, damn days.

I'd been fine on Sunday. Well, mostly fine.

I'd been a little annoyed that Dax hadn't at least checked in to make sure that I made it home safe. I didn't think that was too much to ask from the man who told me to stay inside the bar until my car arrived because he didn't want me waiting outside alone. But I'd reminded myself more than once that just because Dax was polite enough to look out for my well-being while we were out together, he had no reason to check on me when he knew it was one of my uncle's drivers taking me home.

Then Monday had passed without a word. No call, no text, nothing to let me know that he was okay. I told myself that I had a right to be worried since he hadn't looked pleased that Cleo had facilitated an unplanned meeting with someone he'd dropped everything – including me – to get to. For all I knew, this mysterious *mutual friend* was someone dangerous. Between the warning Gavin had given me about Dax, and the men at the shop, it wasn't unthinkable that Dax had been walking into a less than ideal situation.

When I woke up this morning and my phone showed the same thing that I'd seen the previous two days, concern and annoyance became irritation bordering on anger. Some of that anger was directed at myself. I'd told myself multiple times that Dax and I weren't dating, that we were just friends, tentative ones at that, but I had no experience with any sort of sex, let alone the casual kind. I'd always thought that I'd be able to do the whole friends with benefits kind of thing because I was good at keeping my emotions in check.

I'd just never encountered anyone like Dax before.

I dressed almost automatically, choosing casual jeans and a high-necked sweater. I'd worn something similar to rehearsal yesterday, thankful that the weather was still cold enough that no one looked twice at my shirt choice. Only I knew the real reason behind my selection had more to do with the still-fading mark than it did with the temperature.

"Stupid son of a bitch," I muttered.

I'd been fairly consistent in the curses I'd sent Dax's way over the past forty-eight hours. There'd been a fair few of them. At some point, I wanted to unload all of them to his face.

I double-checked my hair to make sure it was all contained before heading to the kitchen for breakfast. Gavin and Carrie had left early yesterday, so I'd eaten alone. This morning, however, they were both in the kitchen. Their backs were to me as I entered, and I stopped a moment to watch the two of them together.

Carrie was about five months along, her slightly rounded

stomach a bit more pronounced than usual as she leaned against Gavin. She had one hand on his back, her head resting on his arm. I could hear the low murmur of their voices but couldn't make out any words. I didn't need, or even want, to know what they were saying. It was clearly a private moment between the two of them, and something inside me gave a sharp twist.

I was only nineteen, and I had picked a career that required a lot of focus and work. Intellectually, I knew that casual hook-ups were the smartest way to go. If I was already in a serious relationship, that would've been one thing, but trying to start something wasn't a good idea, and I knew it. I had plenty of time for that later, and if anyone had asked me about marriage and a family, my immediate response would've been to say that I wasn't thinking about either of those things and wouldn't be for years.

Except in that moment, seeing Carrie and Gavin together, the longing that went through me was almost painful. I didn't understand it...or maybe I didn't want to.

I cleared my throat as I moved farther into the kitchen, and Carrie shifted to look back at me and smile.

"Good morning. How did rehearsal go yesterday?"

"Good," I said as I poured myself some coffee.

Carrie and Gavin had both been asleep when I'd gotten back Saturday night, and then they'd been out with Dena, Leslie, and their significant others yesterday, so this was the first opportunity for questioning. I was just glad that Carrie hadn't started off with a question about Dax.

I decided to try to keep the conversation away from the one person I didn't even want to be thinking about. "Todd's meeting me here so we can go in together."

"I like him," Carrie said as she moved away from Gavin to take a plate of scrambled eggs over to the table. "The two of you certainly get along well."

"We do," I agreed. "To be honest, I was a little worried about what it would be like, going into auditions here, working with other people who were trying to do this professionally." I topped off my coffee and took the plate Gavin held out.

"I thought you did this sort of thing back in DC," Gavin said as he joined us.

"I did, but it wasn't the same." I kept my voice bright, wanting to keep the conversation on track. I could feel Carrie's eyes on me, and I knew if I slipped the slightest bit, she'd want to know why. "Most of the people I knew in the theater circuit were either only doing it for fun, or they were already established in local circles. I knew when I came here, it would be a lot more competitive."

"And it's not?" Gavin asked.

"It is," I said. "But this cast is great. No divas. Everyone's all about coming together to make *Collide* the best off-Broadway production possible."

The best part about talking with them about *Collide* was that I didn't have to force myself to sound like I was enjoying it, or make things up. I really did love the cast, and they really were great people. Todd was my favorite, but everyone else was amazing too.

"Have you got to meet Todd's boyfriend yet?" Carrie asked.

I shook my head and grabbed two more bites before I answered. "Hiram doesn't get back from his trip until this weekend."

A few minutes of silence fell over us as we all focused on our breakfast. I kept my head down, eyes on my plate. I needed my mind clear, my attention undivided. Our first read-through had been yesterday, and we were actually getting on the stage today. I couldn't let myself get distracted by anything.

"Are you planning on doing anything after rehearsal?"

Carrie's casual tone didn't fool me, so I played dumb. "Todd and I might go out to eat afterwards, but we won't be out late. It will be a busy week."

"You're not planning on–"

Before she could get the question out, the buzzing of the intercom saved me.

"Todd's here." I carried my things over to the dishwasher, then grabbed my bag and coat.

"Bryne."

I turned back as Carrie said my name.

"You know you can come to me with anything, right?"

I nodded and gave her my best "I'm absolutely terrific" smile, avoided looking at Gavin as I walked out. I pulled on my coat even though I knew I had a ride waiting. I greeted Todd with a smile and a hug, then slid into the car. He was already talking about a conversation he'd had with Hiram last night.

"...so then Hiram tells me that one of his ex's called him to ask if they could work on a project together. Of course, Hiram said no, but then he said he felt like he had to call and tell me right away. When I asked why, he said that he didn't want to hide anything from me..."

Todd's voice faded into the background as the image of Dax and Cleo made its way to the front of my mind. Neither one of them had said that they'd dated, but I wasn't an idiot. It didn't matter that Dax had said he didn't want a relationship. Cleo hadn't been a one-night stand. Not if they had a "mutual friend."

And that was when it hit me.

There was one possibility that I hadn't considered. Cleo could have been a one-night stand, and she could have an excellent reason for telling me to stay away from Dax. Their mutual friend might not have been a *friend* at all. I might've slept with Dax more than once, but I didn't know him. Not really. It was entirely possible that this *friend* was a child.

His child.

I let out a slow breath and blinked back the tears that burned my eyes. I needed to pull myself together and not worry about things that I didn't have the ability to deal with right now. And that pretty much summed up Dax entirely.

I forced a smile and turned to Todd. "Would you mind running through act one, scene three with me? I'm not sure I have the timing right."

And with that, I put Dax out of my mind and focused on what I'd come here to do.

Two fucking days.

Two mother-fucking, long-ass days.

I hadn't seen or talked to Bryne since she'd walked back into the club without me Saturday night, and it'd been two of the longest days of my life. I'd spent Sunday at home with my mom, then worked a twelve-hour day yesterday. Today, I was scheduled to work a normal eight-hour shift instead of another twelve, and I was starting to wish I'd asked for the longer shift.

I couldn't stop thinking about Bryne.

And it wasn't just thinking about the sex either, though there was plenty of that, including a long shower last night where I'd let myself relive every naked moment we'd had together. I'd come harder jacking off to her than I had with any other actual woman I'd ever been with.

I would've tried telling myself that it was because she was so hot or because she was new, but I'd spent too much time thinking about her in non-sexual ways to be able to sell that lie.

Wondering what she was doing. What she was thinking about. If she thought Cleo and I were together. How I could reassure her that I wasn't interested in Cleo. How things were going with her play rehearsal.

And that, of course, made me think about Todd. While I hadn't gotten details of what happened between the characters he and Bryne played, I knew they were the leads, and there was some romance. Which meant there was probably at least one kiss between them.

That particular thought was driving me crazy at the moment. Bryne told me that Todd was gay, but a little voice in the back of my mind kept whispering that Todd could've lied. He wouldn't have been the first man to tell a woman he was gay in an attempt to get in her pants. The whole "you could turn me" thing worked pretty well for some guys.

"Something wrong, Dax?"

My head jerked up to find everyone glaring at me. "No, I'm good. Keep going."

The dirty look Georgie threw my way said he didn't believe a word of it, but he wasn't going to call me on it in front of the other guys. He may have been Booker's second in command, but he knew better than to try to push me around. It was always a toss up whether I'd ignore him or push back.

And he didn't want me pushing back.

"Like I was saying, we're going to be moving the product through the bikes we get in from the people Booker's got lined up."

I resisted the urge to reach over and smack the back of Georgie's head like I had when we were younger. He needed to stop talking like that, or I couldn't be held responsible for what I did. *Product.* I almost snorted a laugh. Booker wanted to start moving coke, so I wanted to be discreet, but I knew Georgie. He'd be running his mouth all over the place about it, trying to sound like a badass. He was talking like this because he thought it made him sound big.

"How much we gonna have?" The new guy asked the question I was sure we were all thinking.

"Five hundred kilos."

The guy we all called Force let out a low whistle and everyone else looked impressed.

I tried not to curse out loud.

Five hundred kilos of cocaine? What the hell was Booker thinking?

Except I didn't really have to ask that question. I knew what Booker was thinking. There was money in moving coke, and he wanted a piece of it.

"Where's he gettin' it all?" Force asked. "I don't know no one 'round here who'd sell that much to someone new."

"Who said we're getting it from here?" Georgie shot back.

This was the part I knew I needed to pay attention to.

"Booker's got a cousin in Jersey. Julius something. He's a dealer with some serious connections." Georgie reached into his pocket and pulled out a joint. He lit it, took a long drag, then leaned back in his chair. He was really enjoying himself.

"So we're gonna buy it from this Julius guy?" the new guy asked.

Georgie shook his head, and the slow smile that curled up his mouth set my teeth on edge. "Nope."

That didn't sound promising.

"Booker's got us going around his cousin? That doesn't sound too smart."

I was glad Force asked it so I didn't have to. He was in the gang, so while it might not have been a good idea for him to question the boss, it was a hell of a lot better than me doing it. The less I involved myself in any of this, the better.

"Naw," Georgie said. "Julius told Booker that he's got a seller sitting on five hundred kilos and wants to get rid of it at a discount. We're gonna buy it from him."

Once again I was struck with the desire to hit him. He knew how this was all supposed to go, and he was dragging it all out on purpose. Part of me even wondered if he was doing it because I was here. He was always trying to one-up me. Had since we were kids.

Georgie had grown up on the same block as me, but he came from a shit family. I might not have known who my dad was, but Georgie had it worse with his dad around. I never got the full story, but I'd seen Georgie with enough black eyes as a kid to know that his old man was a piece of work, and his mom wasn't much better. Between that and the fact that most of our peers respected me but not him, things between us had always felt more like a competition than a friendship.

I knew half the reason he'd gotten me hired here was because that put him over me, and he could show how he had power in his gang while I didn't. Now that Booker had pulled me into things, Georgie would probably pull more of this alpha male shit like he had something to prove.

"So we're going to Jersey to buy this coke, bringing it back here, and then putting it in car and bike parts so we can get it to Booker's dealers?" Little Eddie, the quietest of the bunch, put it all together in one question.

"We gettin' paid to get it?" the new guy asked. "Cuz if we get caught runnin' that much shit, we're fucked."

I didn't say it, but I was thinking the same thing. Booker hadn't given me much detail, only that if I wanted to keep my job, I was going to do this. There'd also been the implication that living was also one of the things on the line if I backed out.

"Yeah, we're getting paid," Georgie said, his voice sharp.

He didn't like being questioned, especially when he was in charge of a job. He wanted people to follow him like they did Booker. No questions. Unwavering loyalty. The sort of respect that made people not want to cross him. The problem was, he wasn't a leader. Booker wasn't a good guy, but he was a leader. He had the type of presence that made people pay attention when he walked into a room. Georgie had never been like that. He was a hot-head. Liked to run his mouth but could rarely back anything up if it required more than beating the shit out of someone weaker than him.

"How much?" the new guy asked.

I didn't like the glint in Georgie's eyes. Last time I'd seen him give someone that look, the guy had pissed blood for two weeks, and his hand still didn't work right. Like I said. Hot-headed.

"Enough." He dropped what was left of his joint on the floor and ground it out with the heel of his boot. "Booker's got it all worked out what we all get. If you want exact numbers, you can ask him."

The kid's eyes widened. Looked like he had some brains after all.

I still wanted to know exactly how much, but I did know enough about Booker to know that he didn't rely on violence for everything. He had no problem paying his people enough for jobs that they stayed loyal.

A sick feeling settled over me. I liked to think of myself as someone who couldn't be bought. Sure, I did some stupid shit, but it was always my choice. And, yeah, sometimes I had to do things I didn't like, but there was always a good reason. I just hadn't considered money a good reason to do anything this stupid.

As much as my mom and I struggled, I'd promised myself I wouldn't do anything that would take me away from her, no matter how pissed I was or how tight things got. But then she got hurt, and money became even more of a problem. Working at Club Privé had kept our heads above water, but now I didn't have that coming in. I hadn't told my mom yet that I'd gotten fired. Carrie was working hard to get my mom what she deserved from her no-good boss. I didn't want Mom getting after Carrie and finding out about Bryne. Not like that.

Getting paid for moving some coke from one place to another didn't sound like such a bad deal. It wasn't like I'd be out selling it to neighborhood kids or anything like that. If I didn't go, the other guys would do the job anyway, and I'd miss out on the money without changing anything.

I knew I was trying to justify accepting the job, but knowing it didn't stop me. I didn't need an exact number to know that it'd be more than I made here. More than enough to fool my mom into thinking I was still at the club, for a while anyway. I didn't know exactly how much everything cost because my mom wouldn't tell me – she said she didn't want me to worry – but I wasn't blind. I could read "late notice" on almost every bill that came in the mail. We couldn't afford to fall any further behind.

"How come Booker don't have us dealing it? Seems like it'd be cheaper." Force scratched his chin, a thoughtful expression on his face. "And we wouldn't need to mess with any of the bikes or cars."

I was wondering the same thing, but for a completely different reason. Force and the other guys were probably thinking they could make more that way. I didn't want to give Booker any ideas. Becoming a dealer was way too risky.

Besides, if I got caught, it'd kill my mom.

Even as I thought it, another face came into my mind. Bryne. She knew I didn't come from a good background, and she'd overlooked our differences so far. I couldn't even imagine what she'd do if I got arrested for dealing cocaine. She'd probably hate me for making her look bad. She had big plans for her future, but none of them included scandals. Especially not from someone like me.

I didn't think I could do this.

The realization shocked me enough that I almost missed Georgie's answer.

"Booker says it's safer this way. No shit kept around here for long. Money goes through the business so it all looks legit."

"And if we all quit working here, and Booker has to hire a bunch of new people, it's gonna look suspicious," Little Eddie said. "I got a friend in Chicago who got his whole meth operation busted because he wasn't careful."

"When are we going?" Force asked.

"Maybe tomorrow, day after at the latest," Georgie said.

"We're making it up to look like we're going to the junk yard to find spare parts."

Shit. My stomach lurched. Part of me had hoped we'd have a week of planning so I'd have time to figure a way out of it. I had to be smart about it. Come up with a good reason for Georgie to tell me to stay back. But if this was happening in the next day or two, I'd have to flat-out refuse, and I knew Georgie would never take that for an answer. He'd make me go see Booker.

The smart thing would be to do it. Keep my head down, take the money, and then tell Booker that I was out. That I couldn't risk something happening to my mom.

It wasn't Mom I was thinking about though. She loved me unconditionally. It'd hurt her if she found out about any of this, but I'd never lose her love. Disappointment was bad, but she wouldn't turn her back on me.

Doing this meant risking Bryne. I had no claim on her, nothing to hold her to me if things went south. I already knew I wasn't good enough for her, and I kept hoping she wouldn't realize it. If I got caught with coke, she'd know it for sure, and nothing I could do would bring her back.

My head started to hurt. I didn't want this, any of it. I didn't want to be torn up over a girl. I didn't want to be forced into doing something illegal and stupid. I didn't want to worry about getting evicted if I couldn't come up with enough money.

But even as I listed all the things I didn't want, I knew there was one thing I needed more than anything else.

I needed to see Bryne. Needed to know if she would be worth risking everything for. If seeing her would give me the courage I needed to refuse Booker and the money he was offering. Most of all though, I just needed her. I couldn't explain it, didn't want to even think about it, but it was the truth. No matter what I kept telling myself, I knew that, for good or bad, we'd been connected from the moment she stepped into this shop.

I might've been the lead female role in *Collide*, but I was also the youngest. Actually, I was the youngest in the entire cast. Not that there were a lot of us. *Collide* had a cast of only five. Todd, me, August Dumont, Ofelia Makula, and Eolan Iwa. It was essentially a love story at its core, but it wasn't some sweet, feel-good sort of thing, which I loved. The five of us played a cast of characters brought together by tragedy. Todd and I were the couple who fell in love despite the circumstances. August played a professional athlete whose career was ruined. Ofelia's character lost her fiancé, and Eolan was the one trying to make it all better.

On the surface, it seemed fairly simplistic, but the writer had a beautiful, subtle style that drew out all sorts of nuances in the characters...if we were good enough to bring them to life.

"You're brilliant as Gretchen," Todd said for the second time in the last five minutes.

"I'm just worried I won't be able to do her character justice." I sat down with a sigh.

We'd done a basic blocking this morning, then broken for lunch. Before we left, the director announced that we'd be doing a full rehearsal when we got back, and it was then that I started freaking out.

"This is the first time you've done original material, isn't it?" Todd asked. "The stuff you did in DC was all like Shakespeare and Tennessee Williams and all that, right?"

I nodded as I rubbed my temples. I was starting to wonder if I could handle the pressure that came with this sort of life. I could take being on stage, the pressure that came with memorizing, and having people watching me. All of that was fine. It was the pressure of such a small cast and such a complex character. Of knowing that the writer would be watching, and I couldn't let them down.

That wasn't something one had to worry about when doing *Much Ado About Nothing*.

And that wasn't even taking into account all of the shit going on in my personal life.

A pair of strong hands came to rest on my shoulders, then Todd dug his fingers in as he began to massage my shoulders and neck.

"Damn, Bryne. These are some serious knots."

"Be honest, Todd," I said. "Do you really think I can do this?"

"Yes," he answered without hesitation. "And remember, it's not just you. There are five of us, and we'll make *Collide* so good that it'll make the move to Broadway with all of us."

I laughed, feeling that take as much of the tension out of

me as Todd's massage was doing. "You really don't lack for confidence, do you?"

"Nope."

I moaned as his fingers pressed against a particularly tender spot in my neck. "You're really good at that. Does Hiram know how lucky he is?"

"I think so," Todd said. "But you should probably make a point of telling him anyway."

I smiled and closed my eyes, letting myself relax. It was odd how easily I trusted Todd. I'd known him for less than a month, and I had no problem being alone with him in the men's dressing room, my eyes closed, his hands kneading my tight muscles. Part of it, I knew, was because I didn't feel any romantic pressure from him, but that wasn't all of it. I doubted I would've trusted a woman this quickly.

I wasn't aware that I was falling asleep until just before I slipped into a dream, and then I was too far gone to stop.

I stretched out on my stomach, eyes closed. The sun was warm on my body, but not as warm as the hands moving across my skin. I knew his touch so well, knew him so well. I could practically see him etched on the backs of my eyelids. I knew every line of his face, the exact shade of cobalt his eyes were. We'd spent years exploring each other's bodies, learning every dip and curve, but even now his touch made every inch of me throb and pulse with desire.

I rolled over onto my back, and his hands skimmed over my bare breasts, rough palms to sensitive nipples. I moaned, arching my back up into his touch. He chuckled, and I opened my eyes. The heat and passion that I met in his gaze sent a flood of arousal through me.

He pushed my breasts together and lowered his head, flicking his tongue back and forth across my nipples until they hardened. I reached up and buried my hands in his hair, letting myself enjoy the soft, silky strands between my fingers. I held his head against me, gasping as his teeth scraped my sensitive skin.

"Dax." I squirmed under him, his hard body a welcome weight. "Dax, please."

"Please, what?" His fingers skimmed across my stomach.

"Dax." I nearly whined the word.

He made a chiding noise, then shifted so that he gripped both of my wrists in one of his hands. He pulled my arms above my head, pinning them there. His other hand danced over my breasts, between them, down to my bellybutton.

"Please what, Bryne?"

How I loved the sound of my name on his tongue. The way he spoke those words, pushing me to say what I wanted from him. He was my first lover, my only lover, and he continued to inspire and excite me. He encouraged me to explore, to talk about the things I wanted. Nothing was off-limits, nothing too intense.

"Fuck me, Dax," I begged. "I need you inside me."

"What do you need?"

I glared at him, knowing what he wanted me to say. "Your cock. Is that what you want me to say?"

He grinned, the casual ease of his expression making my stomach flip. It had taken time to get him to let down his guard, and it was still only in the most intimate of moments that he was totally open.

"Say it, Bryne." He reached down to grasp his thick erection, moving his hand in slow, sure strokes up and down. "Tell me what you need."

I struggled against his grasp, wanting to get my hands on him. Mark his skin with my nails to make sure everyone knew he was mine. My eyes fell on the silver stud through his nipple, and my mouth watered. I loved the feel of the metal in my mouth, loved teasing it with my tongue. I'd once made it a goal to have my mouth all over Dax's gorgeous body, and now I wanted to do it again.

"Bryne." His voice held a warning note, and a thrill went through me.

I knew what that meant. If I didn't answer his question, there would be consequences. A spanking with his bare hand, perhaps. A flogging where soft leather strips would come down on some of the most sensitive parts of my body. Maybe he'd fuck my mouth, taking his pleasure there and leaving me wanting until he decided I'd had enough. He might decide to take my ass and force me to come without touching my clit. Pinch and twist my nipples until they were swollen and deliciously sore. Take me to the edge so many times that I sobbed with need.

Every punishment sounded better than the last.

I gave him the coy smile I'd discovered as Dax and I had been exploring our sex life. His eyes narrowed as his fingers flexed around my wrists.

"I need to be punished."

The words had barely left my mouth, and Dax was flipping me onto my stomach. I let out a startled yelp, and that earned me a sharp slap on my ass before Dax yanked my hips up until I was on my knees. The hand between my shoulder blades kept my head down as he pushed my knees far enough apart to leave me completely exposed.

Despite how awkward this position felt, I was soaked, eager for him to do whatever it was he wanted with me. A finger ran up my slit, moving from my clit all the way up to my anus. A whimper escaped as Dax pushed his finger into my ass. He hadn't used any lubrication aside from what he'd gathered from me, and it burned. He worked his finger in and out, twisting it until I started to push back.

"Stay!" He emphasized his command with a sharp slap on my ass.

I squeezed my eyes closed and gave myself over to the sensations coursing through me. I shuddered as a second finger joined the first, stretching me before my body was completely ready. I rode the fine line between pain and pleasure, letting Dax control which way I went.

Then, suddenly, his fingers were gone. My body throbbed in anticipation, expecting to feel his cock replacing the emptiness his fingers had left behind. Except it was something else breaching that tight ring of muscle. Hard, ridged, and almost as thick as Dax's cock, I couldn't figure out what he was now working in and out of my ass, only that it wasn't one of our usual toys.

"How about that?" His tone was almost conversational. "Just about anything can be a sex toy."

"Dax—"

Another smack on my ass, this one hard enough to make me gasp. My whole right cheek was hot and stinging now, and I decided I didn't care what Dax was using. He twisted whatever it was, pushing the unyielding object even deeper, and I groaned.

When the head of his dick brushed my entrance, my eyes flew open. He didn't give me a chance to process before he slammed into me and I screamed. I was too full, stretched too tight. My voice gave out, my throat raw, and I still couldn't stop. He was relentless, his thick shaft opening me wide with each stroke even as my muscles fluttered around the object in my ass. I could feel the orgasm building inside me, and it was bigger than anything I'd ever felt before.

I was so close, ready to tip over the edge—

"Bryne!"

I was shaking, and it wasn't because I'd come. I opened my eyes to see Todd looking down at me, a strange expression on his face.

"You've only got about five minutes to get something to eat, and then we have to head back in."

I sat up, my body tight and aching. My face was flushed, pussy throbbing. I wasn't sure if it was worse to wake up before I got to come, or if it would've been worse to know that I came in my sleep...in front of my friend.

"Thanks," I muttered, running a hand through my hair.

Todd started to walk away, but then paused and looked back at me. "You were dreaming about him, weren't you?"

"Bite me."

Todd laughed, his eyes sparkling. "You know, Bryne, if the sounds you were making are any indication of how Dax is in real life, don't let him get away."

As Todd left me alone in the room, his words echoed in my head. My dream hadn't been based on anything Dax and I had done, and the ease I'd felt wasn't even close to how we were together now. I wanted to believe that we could have all of that together, but I knew real life rarely lived up to expectations. Dax and I were so different that I was starting to think that the short time we'd been together was longer than we had any right to expect.

I'd never been the sort of person who gave up on what I wanted. I always fought for it.

I just didn't know if Dax was worth fighting for.

It took more effort than I liked to get back into my character's head for practice, but after the first couple minutes, I felt more like Gretchen than like myself. Considering how well I liked the character, and how much I didn't want to be in my head right then, it was a good thing.

Things fell into a wonderful rhythm between the five of us as we began to find our characters within ourselves, and how those characters related to each other. It was interesting, I thought, how we could all get along so well as ourselves, and then have such great chemistry playing characters who were so different than we really were.

Pretty much the only thing Gretchen and I had in common was our age. She was a surfer girl from California, from a big, laid-back family. Sweet and shy and innocent. Soft-spoken. She grew over the course of the play into someone with some backbone, but it was a real challenge portraying someone who had to grow into a characteristic that I'd always had.

By the time the director finished giving us our notes on the day, it was late afternoon, heading toward evening, and I was feeling better than I had at the beginning of the day.

"Want to grab something to eat?" I asked Todd as we picked up our things.

"I would," he said, "but Hiram's supposed to be calling in a half an hour so we can make plans for when he's coming home."

"It's hard being away from him, isn't it?" I pulled on my coat.

"Harder than I thought it would be," he admitted. "Hiram and I have been dating for a while, and we're exclusive, but we haven't talked about moving in together or anything like that. We've both always liked having our own space."

"But now?" I prompted when he fell silent.

A sweet sort of expression came over his face. "Now, all I can think about is seeing him again and how much I hated us being apart." He ran a hand through his hair and sighed. "I don't want us to have to make plans to do things together whenever we can manage it. I want our being together to be the norm, and time apart to be infrequent."

"I think when he gets back, the two of you need to spend some time talking about that."

A shadow passed over Todd's face. "I know. I'm just worried that he won't want the same thing."

I reached out and squeezed his hand. "He will."

Todd raised an eyebrow. "And you know this how?"

I smiled. "Because you're totally gorgeous, and one of the kindest, most amazing men I know, and if you were straight, I'd be all over you."

He laughed and threw his arm around my shoulder. "I didn't think I was your type, sweetheart, gayness aside. Don't you usually go for the bad boys?"

My chest tightened. "I wouldn't know about usually, but that's been the case since I've been here."

I pulled out my phone to check on my ride. Ofelia had told us after lunch that it'd started snowing, and the forecast said we should expect a lot more. Snow was beautiful, but I didn't want to be standing around in it. According to the app, the car was just around the corner and would be here in a couple minutes.

"Maybe I should take a page out of your book," I said. "Find someone more than twenty years older than me."

He shot me a grin. "And here I thought you meant you were going to switch teams."

I laughed and shook my head. "Unfortunately, I like dick too much."

Todd burst out laughing. "Me too, hon."

The tension in my chest lightened as I joked with my friend. Things with Todd were so easy and pleasant. I wished it could be like that between Dax and me. That I could know where things stood and not spend my time second-guessing and wondering. This was exactly the sort of thing I wanted to avoid. I just thought that by not being in a defined relationship, it would be different. The thing was, I was pretty sure it had less to do with my inability to keep things casual and more to do with the connection Dax and I had. If it'd been any other guy, I doubt that I would've had this problem.

Except I didn't want another guy.

"Are you going to go find him?" Todd asked as he held open the door for me. "Get some stress relief going on?"

I rolled my eyes and was just about ready to come back with a smart remark when I saw someone leaning against the car waiting for me. I didn't even need a full look to recognize that tall, lean frame. Merely a glimpse was enough to make my stomach flip.

"Bryne?" Todd sounded puzzled, then followed my gaze. "Oh."

"Yeah," I said. "Oh."

"Hey." Dax pushed himself off the car and took a couple steps toward me, stopping just before he was close enough to touch.

"Hey."

An awkward silence hung over the three of us for several seconds before Todd broke it.

"I'll leave you two alone." He gave me a quick hug, taking a moment to whisper in my ear, "Follow your heart, Bryne. If he makes you happy, go for it."

As he walked away, I wanted to tell him that I didn't know if Dax made me happy, but considering Dax was standing right there, it didn't seem like the best time to have that particular conversation.

Dax opened the back door to the car. "Get in."

My eyebrows went up as I bristled at the command. "Excuse me?"

A muscle in his jaw twitched. "Please."

I wanted to say that I got into the car because it was cold and I didn't want to be out in the snow, but that was only a small part of the reason. He'd said *please*. That was some-thing I hadn't expected, not after the strange way we'd left things, and I already had too many questions for him.

I slid into the backseat and kept moving until there was

room for Dax too. The driver glanced in his rearview mirror, his expression unchanging when he saw Dax.

"Where to, Miss Bryne?"

I glanced at Dax, who gave me a very unhelpful shrug. "Can you find somewhere to park until I figure out what we're going to do?"

"Yes, miss."

The window went up without me asking, and I made a mental note to tell Gavin that his driver deserved a bonus. The car began to move, and I turned toward Dax.

"Where have you been?" The question came out harsher than I intended.

"It doesn't matter." He reached out and twisted a curl around his finger. "I'm here now."

"It does matter." I moved his hand away. "I thought we were having a good time, and then this woman comes up, and you're basically blowing me off."

"It wasn't for Cleo."

There was something still guarded about his expression, but I could still hear the honesty in his words.

"Who is she?"

He moved closer, his arm sliding around my shoulders. "I don't want to talk about her."

He bent his head, but I turned away so that his lips brushed against my cheek. He sighed and leaned away.

"We hooked up a couple times, okay?"

I crossed my arms to keep from reaching for him. I wanted answers, and my head knew it was the smart thing to do, but my body just wanted *him*. "Well, considering that she warned me to stay away from you makes me think it was a little more than just hooking up."

That got a real reaction as his head jerked up, his eyes wide for a moment before they narrowed. "She did what?" The question was nearly a growl.

"The second time we..." Heat rushed to my face. "Anyway, the next morning, I was going to meet Todd at Tavern on the Green. A woman I didn't know stopped me and told me to stay away from you. Cleo."

"Did she threaten you?"

Tension radiated off him. "I'm pretty sure her exact words were to 'stay the fuck away' from my man.'"

"I'm not her man." He took my face between his hands, holding me in place as his mouth came down on mine.

The kiss was fierce and deep, something almost desperate as he pushed his tongue between my lips. I leaned into him, my hands moving to clutch the front of his shirt. The taste of him, scent of him, it was more addictive than anything I ever could have imagined. It was like the moment he touched me, nothing else mattered.

When he broke the kiss at last, he didn't pull away. His hands slid down to either side of my neck as he rested his forehead against mine. I kept my eyes closed, unsure if I could handle looking at him just yet. His thumb brushed over the pulse in my throat.

"I've been thinking about doing that from the moment you walked back into the club the other night."

I wanted to ask him why he hadn't kissed me then. Why he'd let me go home and ignored me for days. I didn't though. Something in my gut told me that if I pushed too hard, if I asked too much, I would lose him. I didn't know if I was ready to label what we had, but I did know I wasn't ready for it to be over.

There was one thing I did have to know though.

"The mutual friend Cleo mentioned."

His entire body tensed, and a faint sick feeling curled in my stomach.

"Is it a kid?"

He pulled back, a confused look on his face. "What?"

"Do you and Cleo have a child together?"

The shock on his face was almost an answer itself.

"No!" He stared at me. "What would make you think that?"

I shrugged. "We don't know that much about each other. It's not like that's really a strange question to ask, especially with how secretive Cleo was being."

He shook his head. "I don't have any kids. I swear."

Relief rushed through me. I could handle an annoying ex, and even the crazy back and forth as we figured things out. I just didn't want a kid being involved. Not that I disliked them. I just didn't want to do anything that could possibly hurt a child.

"What about you?" He shot the question back at me. "Any kids?"

"You better hope not." The comment flew out of my mouth before I could stop it. "Shit."

He shifted so that his body was angled toward mine. "What does that mean?"

Shit shit shit shit! I blamed his kiss on making my head too befuddled to remember that I planned on never telling him that he was the only guy I'd ever slept with. I could lie, but I had a feeling he'd know. And he'd never let me not answer at all.

I squared my shoulders and forced myself to keep my head up. I didn't want this to be a big deal.

"The first night we were together was my first time."

"Bryne–"

I held up a hand as I cut him off. "It was my choice, Dax. I knew what I wanted. I wasn't looking for some special, romantic gesture. I wanted good, hot sex, and that's what I got. It's not a big deal."

He gave me a hard look, like he was trying to see if I was just saying what he wanted to hear. After a few seconds, he grinned. "Could've fooled me." His heated gaze ran down my body and back up again. "You're fucking amazing."

The tension that had tightened my shoulders again eased even as I flushed. "Don't think you can sweet talk me into sex in the back of the car. I don't want to explain that to my uncle."

Dax laughed, then reached over to take my hand. "While I'd never say no to getting in your pants, I was thinking more along the lines of dinner and a movie."

I raised an eyebrow and tried to ignore the way his touch sent tingles of electricity through me. "Really?"

"Hey, I'm not saying I won't be asking to fuck you senseless before the night's over. Let's just get something to eat and check out a movie first."

Food, movie, sex. Sounded like a great way to unwind. And I was starting to get the impression that this was how things would go between the two of us for a while anyway. As long as I had that in my head, I would be fine with it.

After all, that's all I wanted. Not a commitment or anything like that. I just wanted to know what to expect.

Nothing more.

TWENTY-THREE
DAX

Seeing Bryne was supposed to make things easier, supposed to help me decide what to do. A part of me was hoping that I would see her, and it wouldn't mean anything. I could tell her that I was just checking up on her, that I wanted to make sure she was okay before I walked away. It wouldn't make me *want* to do the job for Booker, but I'd at least know that I wouldn't be putting my relationship with her on the line. The risk would be worth the reward.

Except the moment she stepped outside, and I saw that guy's arm around her shoulders, I'd wanted nothing more than to tell Todd to get lost. I didn't care if he was gay. I didn't want anyone but me touching her. Hell, it'd taken all of my self control to wait until we were in the car to kiss her.

Considering how much I needed every penny of my paycheck, my suggestion of dinner and a movie wasn't a good one, but I needed to spend time with her. Needed to know if she was worth me passing up a job and potentially – no, definitely – pissing off Booker. I had a lot to lose.

And now I was pretty sure she was one of those things I didn't want to lose.

Things had gone well once I'd gotten over the shock she'd given me, but even now as we sat next to each other in the theater, I found myself going through it again.

A virgin.

I'd always stayed away from virgins. Never wanted the responsibility that I thought would come with being someone's first.

But Bryne wasn't like that. She hadn't acted upset that we didn't wake up together, or that she hadn't met my mother. She wasn't pushing for more time together or whining for a commitment.

Sure, she'd asked me about Cleo, and then surprised me with a question about kids, but I'd been around enough jealous women to know Bryne wasn't like that. She wanted answers but didn't seem put off when I didn't offer details about where Cleo and I had gone or who we'd talked to.

One thing was for certain, I thought as I glanced over at the woman sitting next to me. Bryne Dawkins wasn't like anyone I'd ever met before.

She'd been enthusiastic about sex, unafraid to say what she wanted, but even though I hadn't suspected her of being a virgin, I hadn't thought she'd slept around either. She wasn't naive, but there was definitely an innocence about her. Sweet, but she clearly didn't take shit from anyone.

And the more time I spent with her, the more I wanted. Wanted to talk to her, touch her. Hell, just being near her did something to me. In the past, I'd wanted a woman's body, and afterwards, I was done. Maybe that made me a bastard, but I never promised them anything else. If we danced or ate or talked, it was all foreplay.

With her, it was more. Sure, I wanted to fuck her again, but it wasn't like with other women where I was counting down the seconds until I could get my dick inside her.

As the credits began to run, Bryne shifted against me. I tightened my arm around her, wanting to keep her right where she was. Her head on my shoulder. The scent of her floral shampoo surrounding me. The feel of her soft curves. I was pretty sure she'd fallen asleep at some point during the movie, and I didn't even care that I'd spent money on a ticket she wasn't actually using. I would've bought another one if it meant I got to keep her here with me like this.

She sat up as the lights came on, her cheeks turning pink as she glanced at me. "Sorry. I didn't mean to fall asleep."

"It's okay." I shrugged, determined to keep my tone casual. She didn't need to know how much I liked that she trusted me enough to do that. Trust wasn't something I felt very often. Even less now that I'd lost Carrie and Gavin's.

A little voice in the back of my head spoke up, telling me I should have Bryne talk to them for me, see if I could get my job back. I quickly pushed that aside. I didn't want Bryne thinking I only wanted to be with her to get back in the club, even if it would've helped a lot. Once I told Booker I wouldn't do the job, maybe I'd go see Carrie myself, make things right. I didn't like the idea of Bryne's family thinking I'd treat her bad.

I stood and ran a hand over my face. I needed to quit thinking like that. Bryne and I were having a good time. That was all. Telling Booker no was because of my mom, not her.

She smiled up at me, her eyes still a little hazy with sleep.

Okay, maybe not *only* because of Bryne.

"I need to go to the restroom," she said as we started to walk toward the door. "Splash some cold water on my face."

"I'll wait over there." I gestured toward an out of the way spot. I watched Bryne disappear, then moved over to lean against the wall.

I hadn't been there more than a minute when a familiar voice caught my attention.

"Aren't the two of you sweet?"

I scowled as Cleo sauntered over, wondering how the hell she'd located me here. She seemed to be able to locate me most everywhere, something I'd need to look in to. The bitch looked pretty pleased with herself. She wore far too few clothes for the weather, and swung her hips as she walked, clearly enjoying the stares she was getting.

"What do you want?" I snapped. "Georgie didn't say we were meeting tonight."

"Oh, I'm not here for Georgie." She stepped into my personal space, her breasts pressing against my arm.

I ignored it, knowing a reaction was what she was looking for. "What then?"

"Booker."

My jaw clenched.

"He's worried you're gonna get cold feet."

Fuck. I thought I'd been careful to keep my opinion about the job to myself.

"I'll do what I need to do." That was vague enough that no matter what I did, I wouldn't be lying.

"Good." She glanced toward the bathroom. "Because if you don't, your new little bitch is gonna be the one to pay."

I pushed off the wall, glowering down at Cleo. "What'd you say?" I growled, my hands curling into fists.

"Not me. Booker. He says that if you don't do your job, he'll take it out on her."

A flash of panic went through me, and I drew on my anger to keep it at bay. Cleo could smell fear or anything like it. I couldn't let her go back to Booker saying that his threat had gotten a reaction out of me. Better I make him think I didn't care.

"What? Did you go bitching to him that I didn't want to fuck you, so you think she's something special?"

A wicked smile curved Cleo's blood-red lips. "Yeah, I told him that you were fucking some rich cunt."

I took a step toward her, and she stumbled back. Anger twisted her face, but I could see the embarrassment behind it. "It's no one's business who I fuck, Cleo. And I don't need threats to do my job. You go ahead and tell Booker that I'll be there, but you keep your mouth shut about Bryne."

The glint in Cleo's eyes said she saw more than I wanted her to, but before I could say anything else, she nodded. "Have fun with your girl, Dax, but make sure your head's in the game, or she'll be sorry."

As she disappeared around the corner, I willed myself to calm down. As much as I wanted to go after her, wanted to go find Booker and tell him to stay the hell away from Bryne, I knew that wasn't the smart thing to do. And I had to be smart about it. No matter how much I told myself that this thing with Bryne wasn't anything important, I couldn't stand thinking that she could be hurt because of me.

"I'm ready to go." Bryne wrapped her arm around mine.

"You want me to take a car home, or did you want to go some-where else?"

I looked down at her, saw her open expression. This wasn't some passive-aggressive shit. She really would be okay with whatever I wanted to do. I wrapped my arm around her waist as I made my decision.

"Let's get to a hotel. I want you naked and under me."

I leaned back against Dax while ignoring the look he was giving me. I wasn't an idiot. I knew he didn't have a lot of money, especially since he wasn't working at the club anymore, and he'd already paid for our meal and the movie. I wouldn't make him add a hotel room on top of that.

I wasn't sure if he'd been paying close attention the last time we'd gone to a hotel, or if he'd figured it had something to do with Gavin, but the minute I told the driver where I wanted to go, I'd known we needed to have a little talk.

"Bryne." Dax's voice was tight. "I can't–"

"I know a little bit about your background." I cut him off but still didn't look at him. "But you don't know a lot about mine."

"I don't see–"

"I wasn't raised with money." I opted for the short version since the long one was a bit too personal. We weren't there yet. "But my mom's family has it. After my dad died, Mom and I moved in with her grandparents." A faint smile curved my lips even as a wave of sadness swept over me. "After Nana and Papa passed, I inherited everything."

Seconds passed by as he absorbed this new information. Finally, he asked, "How much is everything?"

"Enough," I said. "The room's on me."

"Like hell it is."

Great. Petulant Dax wouldn't be any fun. I needed to nip this in the bud, or there'd be no point to getting a room.

"You're not my boyfriend." I kept my tone gentle, but firm. "We were really clear about that, right? We aren't in a relationship, which means you can't pull the money card. I want to go here, so I'll pay for it."

I expected an argument, and when I finally glanced at him, he didn't look happy. Before he could say anything though, I decided to play dirty. I reached over and ran my hand up his leg. The muscles under my hand tensed, then he sucked in a breath as I brushed my hand across his crotch.

The heat in his eyes as he turned toward me made my stomach clench, but I didn't back off. I wanted him so much that it almost hurt. If I had to be forward to make him see that the money didn't matter, then that's what I would do. If I had to emphasize the fact that we weren't a couple, I'd do that too.

"You trying to buy me off?"

"Depends," I said.

"On what?"

"On what gets you naked the fastest."

He grabbed the back of my neck and pulled me against him, a wicked grin curving his lips a moment before his mouth came down on mine. His teeth scraped then bit my bottom lip until it throbbed. His fingers dug into me, as if he couldn't get me close enough. I understood the feeling, needing to move until I was straddling his lap, feeling his body hard against and beneath mine. I dug my nails into his chest, my other hand in his hair even as he fisted mine, using it to turn my head, deepen our kiss. His other hand splayed across the small of my back, his heat burning through my clothes. The strength I felt in his fingers made me shiver.

Todd was strong, and his touch had been pleasant. But nothing more than that. The relief I'd felt from his massage wasn't sexual at all. With Dax, every touch was sexual. Every touch made me crave more, made intimate parts of my body throb and ache. I thought I knew what it was like to be turned on, to have my body need release.

And then I met Dax and realized I'd known nothing.

I ground down on him, my moan mingling with his. We had layers between us, but the memory of him inside me was so strong that I could almost feel it.

"Miss Bryne."

Dax growled at the man's voice, his hands gripping me possessively. I might not have been his girlfriend, but his reaction left no doubt that I was his, if only for right now.

"Miss Bryne, we're here."

Here? It took me another moment for the statement to get through, and only then did I break the kiss. Dax made an annoyed sound.

"We're at the hotel." My voice was breathless, raw. "The quicker we get checked in, the quicker we can get to a room."

I heard the driver laugh as Dax pulled me after him, barely taking the time to shut the door. I didn't pay much attention to it because as soon as we stepped inside the lobby, Dax's hand went from holding mine, to sliding around my waist and under my shirt. My stomach muscles fluttered as his fingers caressed my ribcage.

By the time we practically fell out of the elevator and into our hallway, everything about me was burning. Butterflies in my stomach. Arousal throbbing between my legs. Skin tingling. My hands shook as I unlocked the door, and none of it was because of nerves.

"Clothes off," Dax ordered as he reached for the back of his shirt, pulling it over his head. "I need you naked. Now."

He finished first, crowding into me even as I was still trying to get out of my bra. He picked me up and my legs went around his waist, only the thin fabric of my panties keeping us from full skin-on-skin contact. He grabbed my hair, yanking it back so he could have access to my neck. Teeth and tongue on my skin made me moan and gasp, commanding my attention until he dropped me onto the plush armchair just a few feet from the door.

"Hands up. Grab the back of the chair."

I did what he said without question, the edge to his voice making me shiver. If this was what it was like to be with someone who was dominant in the way people at Club Privé used the word, then I definitely needed to explore that option.

Dax knelt down, his cock already hard, curling up toward his stomach. He didn't look like he was going to just slam right into me though. The glint in his eyes said that he planned on making this memorable.

"Keep your hands there." He hooked his fingers into the waistband of my panties and pulled them off, tossing them over his shoulder without a second glance. "No touching."

I nodded, wondering if this was what he'd be like at the

club, in one of those special rooms. I made up my mind to talk to Carrie, not only about getting Dax his job back, but also about seeing if there was some sort of compromise we could make about me being allowed into the club to play.

His eyes stayed on my face as he grasped my ankle and lifted it. To my surprise, he draped it over the arm of the chair. When he picked up my other leg and moved it to the other arm, it took everything I had not to drop my hands to cover myself. He'd gone down on me before, but that sort of contact was different than being exposed like this.

"You have amazing tits," he said as he cupped my breasts in his hands, his thumbs brushing over my nipples. "Has anyone else gotten to touch them? Play with them?"

The questions caught me off guard, but I didn't even hesitate to answer them. "Kind of." When his eyes narrowed, his gaze moving to my face, I clarified, "The guy I went to senior prom with copped a feel over my dress."

I let out a startled yelp as he pinched my nipples. Hard. He kept staring at me as he pinched me again, then rolled the stinging flesh. The pain was different than anything I'd ever felt. It was similar to when he'd spanked me the other day, but this was rougher. Rougher than I ever imagined I would want. But I did want it. I'd been wet before, but each twinge of electric pleasure sent another flood of arousal to my pussy until I could feel it dripping on the chair beneath me.

I flushed, unsure if the reaction was from being embarrassed or being turned on. Considering the way I arched into his touch, I guessed it was more of the latter than the former.

"So I'm the only man who's gotten to taste them?"

I nodded, not trusting myself to speak. I didn't know what had gotten into him, but I liked it. In fact, I was pretty sure I was more than halfway to something more than like, despite how dangerous I knew that was.

He leaned down and took one aching nipple into his mouth. He sucked hard, not bothering to ease me into it.

"Dax!" I cried out his name when he bit down, just on this side of pain. He repeated the same actions on my other nipple. Suck. Bite.

"Do you want me to stop?" He looked up at me. "All you have to do is say the word. Tell me you don't like what I'm doing and I'll stop."

He would, I knew. He might push me, might be trying things that I'd never tried before, but he would never force me into something I didn't want.

I used my arms as leverage and pushed my breasts up toward him. "More."

My head fell back as his mouth latched onto me again. He alternated back and forth, using fingers and teeth to twist and pull, suction and tongue to torment. My breasts were heavy, pressure coiling tight inside me, working me toward what I knew would be an explosive orgasm. The moment his thumb brushed against my clit, that was it.

Pleasure crashed into me, almost painful in its intensity. I felt Dax's hands on my ankles, holding them down as my body tensed, but it wasn't until I opened my eyes a few moments later, that I realized my ankles were the only places he was touching me, and he wasn't doing anything more than holding me. Instead, he was watching me with something that looked almost like awe.

Before I could become self-conscious, he spoke, "Did any other man ever make you come?"

I shook my head. "Only the men in my head."

He chuckled, but there was something primal and almost dark to the sound. "Good. I don't like the idea of anyone else getting to see you come."

A shiver ran through me, and a part of me even dared to hope that his words meant he wanted to be the only one giving me orgasms for a while. I bit my bottom lip, refusing to even think about anything other than getting to have sex with him. That was enough.

He shifted until he was almost sitting on his heels, then grabbed my hips and yanked me to the edge of the chair. I had about three seconds to feel a bit of friction burn on my back before the sensation disappeared beneath the exquisite pleasure of Dax's tongue buried in my pussy. He kept his hands on the inside of my thighs, keeping me spread wide as he lapped up the evidence of my previous climax and worked me toward another.

I wasn't even aware I'd dropped my hands to Dax's head, trying to hold him against me, until I felt his teeth on my clit. My eyes flew open to see him staring at me. Slowly, I raised my hands back up behind me, and he raised his head.

"Next time, I'll stop and make you suck my cock while I finger you to the edge half a dozen times. You'll be screaming before I decide to let you come."

His breath against my pussy made me shiver.

Or maybe it was his words that did it.

"Say you understand."

"I understand." The words were barely a whisper.

While I desperately wanted to come, a part of me also wanted to know what it would feel like for him to follow through. To have him in my mouth, feel the weight of him, taste him. To be driven to the edge and held there.

Then he lowered his mouth again and took me, screaming, to the edge and over. It was almost brutal, the way he licked around and over and in, then attacking my clit until I came. He didn't let up though, continuing to suck on the swollen bundle of nerves until it was throbbing as much as my nipples.

"Please!" The word tore out of me when I couldn't take anything else.

My body was still shaking when he picked me up and carried me into the bedroom. I moaned as he sat me down, then rolled me onto my stomach, my head at the edge of the bed. Something brushed against my lips and my eyes fluttered open. His cock hovered in front of my face, and I didn't even hesitate to flick out my tongue against the tip, the taste of him bursting across my taste buds.

"Open."

I did as he said, prickles of pain and pleasure moving across my overly sensitive nipples as they rubbed against the bedspread. He slid between my lips, moving across my tongue until he almost went too far. Before I could gag though, he pulled back. I pushed myself up on my elbows to make it easier to breathe, but I didn't touch him, letting him slowly thrust into my mouth. I concentrated on tasting him, running my tongue over the soft skin, learning the feel of him.

He reached down and cupped my chin, his thumb running across my bottom lip. "You have no idea how much I want to fuck your mouth. Make you take me all the way to the root. Feel your throat around me. Watch you swallow every drop, then lick your swollen lips."

I didn't know what turned me on more, his actions or his words.

"But I want that tight cunt more."

He pulled out of my mouth, walked around to the other side of the bed, and grabbed my ankles. I cried out, half in pain, half in pleasure, as he yanked me across the bed. I was pretty sure wearing a bra tomorrow would be excruciating, but it was already worth it.

Even as my toes brushed the carpet, I heard the now-familiar sound of a condom wrapper ripping, and braced myself for what I knew was coming. Being prepared didn't stop me from keening as he slammed into me. There was no tenderness, no gentleness, but I hadn't asked for either of those things. This was passion and desire, the total and complete loss of self and immersion in the animalistic act of two bodies coming together.

And I let myself take it all. Every thrust of his thick cock that stretched me wide and hit me deep. Every dig of his fingers into my hips. Every grunt of pleasure from him. Every wave of ecstasy that washed over me.

I didn't let anything else in, didn't let anything mar what was happening between us. I wanted him, and he wanted me. And as I came for the third time, that was enough. Spots danced in front of my eyes, and I felt the world going gray as he called out my name. I allowed myself a burst of pride before letting the darkness consume me.

I couldn't stop myself from climbing into the bed with her after I cleaned us both up. She passed out right after she came – something I wouldn't deny brought a burst of pride – and hadn't even stirred when I ran a damp washcloth between her legs. My stomach clenched as I looked at her pink, swollen pussy, at her delicious nipples. I'd never thought there was anything specifically appealing about fucking a virgin, but I couldn't stop myself from thinking about how I was the only man who'd ever put my mouth on her, was inside her.

So far.

The two words popped into my head, and a flare of anger went through me. I pushed it all down as I pulled the blankets over us and wrapped my arms around her. I couldn't stay all night, no matter how much I wanted to, but I would take what I could get. She made a soft noise and snuggled back against me. My cock gave an interested twitch, and I briefly considered rethinking my decision not to stay. I could let her rest for a bit, then wake her up nice and slow. Slide my fingers between her legs until I coaxed an orgasm out of her. Then take her from behind, maybe even push my thumb into her ass, see if it was as tight as I thought it would be.

The urge to keep her around so that I could take her ass was stronger than ever. To be the first man to have her in every way possible. I refused to let myself think of being the only man to have her. That wasn't possible. Especially not after Cleo's visit. Being around me was putting Bryne in danger. Being *with* me would make her an even bigger target.

This was the last time we could be together. The last time I'd get to feel her hot, sinful mouth, or sink inside her tight pussy. The last time I would feel her come on my tongue, taste her.

No matter how much I hated it, how sick I felt at the thought of what it would do to her when she woke up and I was gone – again – she was safer away from me. We hadn't made any promises to each other, and while I knew it would hurt for me to leave without a word or note, a clean break was for the best.

She had Todd to help her and comfort her. He was her friend and wouldn't leave her.

And he wouldn't try to take advantage of her either. I could hate knowing how close they were and how much closer they'd get, but at least I didn't have to feel jealous of him doing anything else.

It shook me more than I liked, knowing that I had such strong feelings against anyone who still got to be in her life. And I didn't even want to think about the jealousy. I'd never been jealous of anyone in my life. Definitely not over a woman.

But the woman in my arms wasn't just any woman.

And that was why, as the bedside clock showed midnight, I eased her out of my embrace and climbed out of bed. I dressed quickly and quietly, then walked away without looking back. I didn't trust myself not to give in to the temptation to stay, and that could cost her more than I was willing to pay.

With my gut churning, I left the hotel and headed for the subway, barely feeling the icy wind and shards of frozen rain on my face. I had a job to do, and the first part of that was to make sure that Booker knew Bryne was off-limits.

My mom had told me more than once that I didn't think about the consequences when I did dumb stuff, and I never really thought that was true before. I always thought I knew what I was doing, that I considered the risks. Except now I knew that wasn't right because if I had, I wouldn't have let myself get caught up in Georgie's shit at all. As soon as I discovered the shop was a front for the gang, I should've left. Tried to find work somewhere else. But I hadn't. It wasn't easy work, but it was easier than looking for something else. I had a high school diploma, but that didn't mean shit most of the time, especially if you had as much ink as I did.

Now I had to deal with the fallout, and if that meant staying away from Bryne and risking my ass to go on some drug run, that's what I'd do. Whatever it took to keep Mom and Bryne safe.

New York was called "The City that Never Sleeps," and that was never any more apparent than riding a subway at midnight during the middle of the week. Sure, it wasn't close

198 M. S. PARKER

to as crowded as it would be at rush hour, but there were at least a half a dozen people in my car when I got on. The shop was too far to walk, but it was the best place for me to start looking for Booker. Georgie said the two of them were meeting tonight to finalize details about the job, and I knew that whenever Booker came into the shop, he looked over the books. There was a chance he was still there.

I slumped down in a seat and glowered at the empty space across from me. I should've taken a shower before I left. I smelled like sex...and Bryne. I'd never cared before if the guys knew I'd been fucking someone. Pretty much the only times I ever made an effort to be discreet was when I was working at Club Privé – it might've been a sex club, but Gavin and Carrie had strict standards – and when I was around Mom. Now though, I wished I'd thought to clean up more than just a cursory wipe down. I didn't want Booker knowing I'd just come from being with Bryne, and I sure as hell didn't want anyone thinking about Bryne like that.

I stopped myself before I could follow that line of thought any further. I didn't have any claim on her. She wasn't mine. She'd find some other guy, a better guy. Someone with a good job who she could look good standing beside. Yeah, her uncle could do the whole "bad boy" thing, but Gavin was the sort of guy who could make himself look the part for whatever he wanted. Put him in a suit and tie, and he could have lunch with the fucking mayor.

Put me in a suit and tie, and I looked like a phony. I could look good enough for the basic sort of shit couples did together, but now that I knew she didn't just have some money thanks to Gavin, it was brutally clear that we could never be anything more than this. She and her mom might not be on the best terms right now, but I wouldn't be the one who kept her from going back to that life.

I jerked myself upright as the train started to slow. It'd be an extra block to the shop if I got off here, but I needed it. The cold and the physical activity. It was the only way I could stop myself from going right back to the hotel and trying to figure out a way to make her mine.

My feet and hands felt like chunks of ice by the time I stepped into the shop, but I saw a dim light coming from the office, so it was worth it. Most likely, that was Booker. It could be Georgie, but I could reach out to Booker through him, still letting me get this done before we left for Jersey.

The door was open, but I knocked anyway. It was Booker behind the desk, and there was no point in pissing him off by barging in. What I was about to say would piss him off enough.

"Dax." He looked up. "Come in."

I did, but I didn't sit this time. I wasn't here for a friendly chat. "Cleo gave me your message."

The expression on Booker's face was mild, but I knew better than to trust it.

"Did she?" He leaned back in the chair and it let out a screech that set my teeth on edge.

"I'm doing the job. Leave the girl alone."

Booker's eyes narrowed, and I knew I was toeing the line. I wasn't going to back down though. He didn't respect weakness. I just had to be careful with what he thought my reasons were. If he knew how much Bryne's safety meant to me, he wouldn't hesitate to use her the next time he wanted something from me. He had to think it was in his best interest to forget about her.

"Cleo's a jealous bitch." I hooked my thumbs in my pockets. "Sees me around with some new girl and thinks it means shit."

"But it doesn't?"

I shrugged rather than shaking my head, trying to look as bored as possible. "She was a good enough lay, I went back for seconds. Not enough for anything else."

"You said she was off-limits. Seems a bit risky for you to be telling me what to do for a girl you don't care about."

That's what made Booker more dangerous than Georgie. He was a lot smarter than people gave him credit for.

"Her aunt's a lawyer." I wasn't about to tell him that anyone in her family had any sort of money. He might start getting worse ideas about what he could do with her to get a piece of it. "Nothing big time, but she's got enough connections to make my life hell if something happens to her niece, and she thinks I had something to do with it. I don't need that kind of shit in my life."

He was quiet for a minute, his eyes boring into me like he could figure out what I was thinking. "You're right," he said finally. "We don't need lawyers sniffing around while we're dealing with this. Just make sure you do your part, or I'll find someone you do care about."

I gritted my teeth to keep from saying something stupid and nodded. Even though I was just starting to get feeling back in my hands and feet, I headed for the door. I needed to go home and check on my mom, grab a shower and some clean clothes. Then I'd crash at the shop until after this was done. I didn't want Mom thinking I was up to something, and I sure as hell wasn't going to risk one of the guys showing up at the house.

To keep the people I cared about safe, I needed to stay as far away from them as I could until I figured out what the hell I was going to do once this job was done. And no matter how much I'd tried to keep my distance from her, Bryne was one of those people.

TWENTY-SIX

BRYNE

I was starting to think that waking up alone after sex was normal. Then I remembered that nothing with Dax – or whatever it was we had – was normal, so it wasn't exactly the best comparison to use when trying to figure out how things were supposed to go after sex.

He hadn't left a note. Again, not a surprise.

I rolled my eyes as I stretched my arms above my head. I hadn't bothered to explain that another reason I wanted to come to a nice hotel was that I planned on having a slow morning. Taking a nice, hot shower and ordering room service before I headed into rehearsal. Today was costume fittings, so I didn't have to be in until a little after noon, and I wanted to enjoy being a bit lazy for a couple hours.

At least since Dax's behavior was consistent, I wasn't upset that he left. I knew it didn't mean he hadn't enjoyed himself. And that's all we were. Two people who enjoyed spending time with each other. Right now, I was okay with that. I might not be at some point in the future, but that wasn't something I wanted to think about right now.

A muffled ringing made me jump. Shit. That was Carrie's ringtone. I scrambled out of the bed, hurrying into the sitting area where I'd left my purse last night. I'd forgotten to let her know that I wasn't coming home. She and Gavin hadn't set down any sort of rules or anything for me, but I knew it was polite to let them know where I was.

"Hello?" I managed to answer just before it went to voicemail.

"Bryne, are you with Dax?"

I immediately tensed at Carrie's tone. Something was wrong. I wanted to believe that it was just Carrie being over-protective because she didn't like the idea of me hooking up with Dax, but my gut told me that wasn't the case.

"I was, why?"

"How long were you with him?"

I was starting to get the impression that this was how Carrie questioned people when she was in lawyer mode. I stood, barely aware that I was still naked.

"We met after rehearsal yesterday." I began to pace. "Went to dinner, then a movie." I paused to pick up my clothes. "Then we came here."

"Here?"

"A hotel."

"You're still there?"

"I am." I tossed the clothes onto the bed. "We had, um, sex, and I fell asleep." I wasn't about to tell my aunt that Dax had fucked me until I passed out. "I woke up a couple minutes before you called, and he was already gone."

"Are you okay?"

There was more of the aunt than the lawyer in that question.

"I'm fine." I felt compelled to add, "Dax doesn't stay over."

Heat rushed to my cheeks. The words sounded strange, as if I was trying to defend what Dax and I had done. I didn't need to defend it. We were both consenting adults. And I knew Carrie wouldn't judge me. She wasn't like my mother.

"What time did he leave?"

"I'm not sure." Annoyance crept into my voice. "What's going on, Carrie? I know I should've texted you last night to let you know I wasn't coming home, but what's with the interrogation about where he is now?"

The silence went on longer than I was comfortable with, but Carrie broke it before I could.

"Annabeth Prevot called me ten minutes ago," she said. "Dax's mom. She said he didn't come home last night."

"Maybe she just didn't hear him." Dax had talked a bit about his mom but hadn't mentioned that he lived with her. I'd just assumed he hadn't invited me back to his place because we weren't serious. Now that I knew, though, I really got it. I couldn't imagine bringing a guy back to a place where I lived with my mother.

"She's always up when he gets up for work, and he wasn't there this morning."

I swallowed hard and told my queasy stomach that I'd get something in it after things were straightened out with Carrie and Dax's mom. That's all this was. "Couldn't he have left early?"

"He didn't answer when she called. Three times. Or her texts. And he didn't answer when I called either."

Dodging Carrie's calls made some sense. She'd fired him. I could see not wanting to talk to her without knowing what it was about, and I knew something about ignoring a mother's calls.

But not when she called three times in a row, texted, and had someone else call. No matter how much the two of us argued, I would've wanted to make sure nothing was wrong.

"Shit," I whispered as I closed my eyes. "Did she try calling the shop?"

"No one's answering there either. And the 'find my phone' app he usually keeps on for her to check on him is off. He never turns it off because he doesn't want her to worry." Carrie sighed. "Annabeth is worried that he's in trouble...or that he's done something stupid."

Even as little as I knew about Dax, I was pretty sure that it was a matter of him doing something stupid that would get him into trouble.

I just hoped he wasn't in it yet.

I was willing to accept that we weren't anything more than friends who had sex, but I wasn't willing to lose him completely because he was an idiot. I was going to find him, and then I would kick his ass for making me worry.

THE END
Club Prive continues in *Enticed (Club Prive Book 12)*, available now. Turn the page for a free preview.

PREVIEW: ENTICED (CLUB PRIVE 12)

ONE

BRYNE

I never considered myself to be one of those people who had a temper or made rash decisions. Even if something looked impulsive – say, losing my virginity to a guy I barely knew – chances were, I'd thought about it beforehand. And I didn't get angry easily. Sometimes I snapped at people or raised my voice, but I wasn't the sort of person prone to shouting matches or violence.

But right now, all I wanted to do was find Dax and hit him.

Hard.

When I'd woken up alone less than an hour ago, I wasn't surprised or upset. That just seemed to be how he did things. If we were in some sort of relationship that extended past sex, it might've been an issue, but we weren't, so it wasn't. Then Carrie called to ask if I knew where Dax was because he hadn't gone home last night.

Now, I was mentally cursing him as I pulled my curls back into a messy bun. Not only had he not gone back to his place, he wasn't answering his phone or responding to any texts, and his mom was worried. And since I was the last person to see him, Carrie wanted to talk to me in person. Which meant I was about to meet Dax's mother with wet hair while wearing yesterday's clothes.

Needless to say, I wasn't in the best of moods when I went out into the brutal cold to wait for my car. Carrie had already contacted the on-call family driver, but I still had to wait a couple minutes before he arrived. My teeth were chattering, and my hair felt like ice as I climbed into the backseat. As we began to move, I let myself start to think about all the things I'd pushed aside while I showered and dressed.

Things like Carrie and Dax's mom being worried that he was in trouble. The sick feeling I got in my stomach when I thought about him not wanting to tell me about the *mutual friend* he and Cleo had gone to meet earlier this week. The gut reaction I had to his friends at the shop.

I didn't know if Georgie or those other guys had anything to do with where Dax was or why he wasn't taking his mother's calls, but they were the first people I thought of when Carrie said that she was worried.

No, that was a lie. They weren't the first who came to mind. Cleo was. They'd hooked up in the past, and no matter what he said to me about it being over, she clearly hadn't accepted that. I didn't want to consider her being a factor because I didn't want to think that he could've gone with her willingly. At the same time, I seriously doubted she could've forced him. I didn't see Dax being the kind of guy who got intimidated by a gun or knife.

Unless she hurt him, and the reason he wasn't answering the phone was because he *couldn't*.

I wasn't sure which was worse. Thinking that he could've gone with her because he wanted to, or thinking that she'd hurt him badly enough that he was unable to answer his phone. I supposed he could've had another meeting that he didn't want to talk about, but that wasn't a good option either.

I closed my eyes and rubbed my temples. I'd felt great when I woke up. Okay, a little sore considering the sex Dax and I had last night hadn't been even close to gentle. My nipples were so sensitive that the pressure from my bra was almost painful, and the low throbbing between my legs reminded me both of how hard he'd driven into me, and how much I'd been stretched by his delicious cock.

"Dammit, Dax," I muttered as I pulled out my phone to see if he'd responded to my voicemail or text. Still nothing. "Answer your damn phone."

"Did you need something, miss?"

I jerked my head up, startled. I'd forgotten I wasn't actually alone. While there was a partition that could separate the front from the back, providing some privacy, I hadn't asked the driver to put it up, and now he was giving me a concerned look.

"I'm fine," I lied. "How much longer?"

"About ten minutes," he said. "It's only a couple miles to Mrs. Manning's office, but the traffic will cost us a few extra minutes."

It was only now I realized that he wasn't taking me home. While I fully intended to get my own place, I'd been in the city less than a month. Since my new-found uncle and his wife didn't mind me using the guest room in their loft, I was taking my time deciding where I wanted to live.

I'd never been to Carrie's office, and if the circumstances

had been different, I would've been intrigued. As it was, I could barely manage basic curiosity about the place where my aunt was practicing law, despite how interesting I found the subject.

She was a divorce attorney before she and Gavin met. Now, she worked against human trafficking. I'd asked how she did that since she was a private lawyer and not a prosecutor like her friend Dena, and she'd explained that she dealt with the civil side of things. Getting solicitation charges overturned so former sex workers could apply for jobs without criminal records. Filing lawsuits against pimps and others who owned or used slaves in order to seize their assets and have them distributed among the victims. She occasionally did other types of lawsuits where people were being taken advantage of, often free of charge. I was already planning on discussing helping fund some of those cases with the inheritance my great-grandparents had left me but hadn't had a chance yet.

If my life continued to be this crazy, I doubted free time was anywhere in my near future. While I was thrilled to be the romantic lead in an amazing off-Broadway production just weeks after moving here from DC, I couldn't deny that everything was happening so fast that it was making my head spin.

And that wasn't even taking the whole Dax thing into account.

"We're here, Miss Bryne," the driver said as the car came to a stop. "Would you like me to stay nearby to take you to rehearsal?"

Shit. Rehearsal. I'd completely forgotten about it. Fortunately, today was all about costume fitting, so I wasn't missing anything this morning.

"I can come back at eleven-thirty if you'd like."

"Thank you," I said. "That would be great."

I gave him a smile before I climbed out of the car, but my heart wasn't really in it. Now that I was here, the reality of the situation was setting in. I wasn't even sure how much I was supposed to be worrying. It wasn't like he was my boyfriend. If I'd had a regular rehearsal today, I doubted I would've been able to call off or even arrive late.

That didn't, however, mean that I would've been able to concentrate, so I was extra glad that I wasn't expected to do anything today that required any sort of concentration. I was also pretty sure that I had the least complicated costume, which meant I shouldn't have to be there too long. My limited experience with the theaters in DC had been enough to know that this wasn't how practice schedules usually went, but I wasn't going to complain. It made things a bit easier.

Well, as easy as this could be.

Since Carrie's law practice consisted of only her, the office was fairly small but nice. When I walked inside, a petite, dark-haired woman was at the coffee maker. She turned and gave me a wide smile.

"You must be Bryne." She held out a hand. "I'm Zoe Masters, Carrie's assistant." After we shook, she added, "Carrie's waiting for you in her office." She gestured toward the door directly behind her.

"Thank you." I gave a light rap on the door, and it opened a moment later.

Carrie looked tired as she stepped aside to let me in, and I didn't think it was the pregnancy. My guess was, the worried-looking woman sitting a couple feet away was the reason for my aunt's exhaustion. Even without the obvious connection, I didn't need Carrie to tell me that I was looking at Annabeth Prevot. Dax had the same dark hair and similar enough features for the relation to be obvious.

"Annabeth, this is my niece, Bryne."

As she raised her head, I saw a pair of eyes that were a little bluer than Dax's, but close enough to make my heart give a painful twist. She managed a weak smile.

"So you're the girl who's been spending so much time with my Dax."

"I am." I wondered how much he'd told her about me, but this wasn't the time to ask. "You still haven't heard from him?"

Annabeth shook her head. "It's not like him." She gave me a hard look. "I'm not naive. I know that Dax isn't an angel. But he's always been protective of me, especially since my accident."

"Accident?" I asked, then remembered Carrie telling me about Dax's mom getting hurt at work, then her company firing her.

"It's a long story," Annabeth continued. "But anyway, Dax has been great, taking care of me. That's why it doesn't make sense that he isn't answering my calls or texts."

I had to admit, she was right. It didn't make sense when she put it all together like that. I'd seen how protective he was with me, and I knew his mother was way more important to him.

"So when you woke up this morning, Dax was gone?" Carrie asked.

The blood rushed to my face, and that earned a soft chuckle from both women.

"It's okay, sweetie," Annabeth said with a better smile than she'd given me before. "I might be a mom, but I'm still a woman. I know how girls look at him, and I'm not foolish enough to think he doesn't look back."

"We were at a hotel last night, and he left before I woke up," I said, not wanting to think about all of the women he'd looked back at. According to something Carrie had said once, he was five years older than me, and I was pretty sure he'd started having sex younger than nineteen, so there were definitely more women than I cared to count.

Annabeth's expression said that she didn't approve, but before I could worry that she was directing it at me, she said, "I taught him better than that."

I wasn't about to tell her that it wasn't the first time he'd done it. I steered the subject in a different direction by bringing up what I hadn't wanted to say over the phone. "Is it possible he's with Cleo?"

Annabeth's eyebrows shot up. "That girl who went to jail for assault?"

I tried not to let her see how much it hurt that she knew who Cleo was. Dax said they hadn't been serious. Judging by the look Annabeth gave me, I wasn't fooling anyone.

"The incident took place near the shop," she explained. "I saw an article about it in the paper, and when I asked him, he told me he knew the girl. I thought she was in jail."

"She got out a few weeks ago," I said. "I actually met her very briefly. They went to see a mutual friend the other night. Could that be where Dax is?"

Annabeth let out a string of soft curses, and I saw the

same intensity in her eyes that I'd seen in Dax's, increasing the likeness between the two of them.

"Do you know something, Annabeth?" Carrie asked.

"No," she said. "But if that girl is involved, it can't be good."

Well, that wasn't what I wanted to hear.

TWO
DAX

I didn't like New Jersey.

Sure, there were plenty of nice people in Jersey, and I was pretty sure there were nice places too. I just never saw any of them.

Like right now, I was in a real shit-hole of a place, wishing I was back home where I belonged. Georgie, Force, Little Eddie, and the new guy whose name I still didn't know were here too. Booker North – the reason we were freezing our asses off – was back in New York.

I stomped my feet to warm them up and tried not to be the first person to say what I thought was pretty obvious. The coke supplier we were supposed to be buying from wasn't coming. Booker's cousin had set the whole thing up, saying he had a supplier who was sitting on five hundred kilos he wanted to move.

Except there was nothing here. No supplier. No coke. Nothing.

"Mother fucker!" Georgie lost it first, screaming the obscenity.

Another string of curse words followed while the rest of the guys and I tried not to look like we were sitting around with our thumbs up our asses. Georgie was a hot-head, but he was Booker's second, or whatever the hell he was called in their gang. He was the one in charge of this job, so he was calling the shots.

I wasn't in the gang, but I worked at the shop that was going to be part of the new drug dealing business Booker was adding to the stolen parts and money laundering they already did. I looked the other way for all that shit, and they let me do my own thing, but Booker decided that I needed to be a part of this. All day I was trying to figure out exactly why, especially since Georgie could be a real bastard when it came to me. Booker had even sent Cleo to threaten Bryne if I didn't go along with it. It wasn't until the new guy started running his mouth about how he was on his second strike and if he got caught he was fucked, that I figured it out.

Once I was a part of it, moving the dope across state lines, hiding it in the car and motorcycle parts, it'd be harder for me to turn them in without getting into trouble myself. It was one thing to work at a business that had some shady shit going on. It was something else to actually be involved in said shady shit.

"What're we gonna do, Georgie?" the new guy asked.

Georgie ignored the question as he pulled out his phone. I glanced over at Force who shrugged. I could tell the other guys weren't really comfortable with me here, but they weren't about to argue with either of the bosses. That was a good way to end up dead.

"Booker." Georgie paced as he talked. "We're here but there ain't nothing or nobody here."

While Georgie's side of the conversation became silent and then random noises of agreement, I took the time to look around. The warehouse was dirty and dark, making it hard to see much, but I was pretty sure it was completely empty and had been that way for a while. The air smelled stale, like a garage that'd been locked up for a long time. The floor was covered with all sorts of shit, but I didn't see any new-looking footprints or any sign that anything had been moved recently. I was no detective, but that didn't sit right with me. Something was wrong.

"Listen up, bitches." Georgie came back over. "Booker's gonna call his cousin, see if we can find out where this motherfucker might be keeping his shit."

"Then we go get it, right?" The new guy again.

Somehow, I didn't think that was all there was to it.

"By any means necessary," Georgie said.

Shit. He'd heard that once on TV and used it whenever he planned on doing something stupid. Stupid plus coke equaled shit hitting the fan, and that was all it took to get me to talk.

"Booker really wants us stealing from a coke supplier?"

Georgie glared at me, but his phone rang before he got a chance to say another word. "Yeah." After a minute of listening, he glared at me and said, "Dax doesn't think that's a good idea."

Fucking traitor.

Georgie held out his phone, and I took it. "Dax here."

"You questioning me?" Booker's voice was cold.

"Do you want us to steal coke from your cousin's supplier?" I figured I'd better know exactly what I was disagreeing with before I did it. Georgie was no stranger to exaggeration.

"And if I do?"

I chose my words carefully. Most people believed Booker was responsible for the mysterious disappearance of the guy who used to own the shop and his two sons. I wasn't going to argue otherwise.

"I'm looking around here, and it doesn't look like anyone or anything's been here in a while." I took Booker's silence to mean I should keep going. "I'm thinking the supplier was trying to set your cousin up or something. Might be a good idea to take some time to plan rather than going in guns blazing."

I didn't have to tell him that would be Georgie's style. Everyone knew it.

"Put Georgie back on the line."

Booker's tone didn't tell me shit about what he was thinking, but I didn't ask. I'd either made my point, or I hadn't. Either way, Booker would make the call, and Georgie would follow it. He wasn't dumb enough to get one order and give another.

When Georgie hung up, he was pissed. "Booker wants us back so we can come up with a plan to go after the dope."

"So we're not doin' it tonight?" Force asked.

"No." He glared at me, and I heard what he wasn't saying. He'd wanted to go, but Booker had vetoed it because of my input.

I refused to apologize for it. If Georgie led us into something blind, someone would get hurt, probably even dead. I might've kept a little distance from the guys, but I didn't want them killed. Not even Georgie. This way, we'd all get back in one piece, and if Booker still wanted to pull some stupid shit, it'd at least be with a plan.

That didn't mean I would go along with it. Waiting to plan meant I'd have more time to figure out how to get out. For now though, I just stuck my hands in my pockets and headed out to the car. It'd been a long day, and we wouldn't be back in the city until late. I just wanted to sleep on the ride home and not have to think about the mess I left.

I'd seen all of the voicemails, missed calls, and text messages. Mom, Carrie, and Bryne. And I'd ignored all of them. While the guys had heard me talk about my mom before, they didn't know I lived with her, and they definitely didn't know that I was still seeing Bryne.

I doubted that would be the case when I got back though. She might not have been mad at me for leaving her last night, but if Mom and Carrie had told her that I wasn't answering any calls or texts, then she knew something was up. I'd fucked up enough that I wouldn't blame her for saying I'd used up my last chance. And even if she wasn't as pissed as she should've been, there was no way Carrie would want me anywhere near her niece now.

I couldn't deny wondering if Mom had met Bryne. And what they'd thought of each other. I was sure Bryne would love my mom. Pretty much everyone did. Mom hadn't met any of the girls I'd been with before, so I had no way of knowing what her thoughts would be about Bryne. If she'd see the same amazing woman I did.

Well, not exactly the same since there was no way she'd know anything about of the sex part of it. She knew I wasn't a virgin, but there were some things a guy didn't talk about with his mom.

S&M was definitely one of them.

I'd never let myself think about taking anyone home to meet her before. I wasn't one of those guys who said I'd never have a girlfriend or anything like that, but I hadn't let myself think that far ahead, especially after Mom's accident. I'd never met anyone who made me want to think that far ahead.

Until Bryne.

As much as I'd insisted she wasn't anything but a good lay, and as many times as I told myself that I needed to stay away from her, she was the only thing I thought about the entire way back to the city. I cursed, knowing I'd have to deal with this sooner rather than later.

I just didn't know how.

THREE

BRYNE

My costume fitting went well, and I loved how easy it made it to slip into character, but I wasn't able to truly enjoy any of it. And it was all Dax's fault. After my fitting yesterday, I'd taken lunch back to Carrie and Annabeth, then went back home to work on my lines. At least, that was the plan. It was almost impossible to concentrate on memorizing anything. I kept thinking about Dax and where he was and what he was doing. Every so often, I'd grab my phone, thinking that I'd missed something. Of course, there was nothing there, and I'd start worrying all over again.

When Carrie came home, I took one look at her face, and she hadn't even needed to shake her head. I'd barely eaten dinner and then spent the rest of the night staring at my ceiling, trying to tell myself that the universe was sending me a sign, telling me to stay away from Dax, that he'd only hurt me.

At one point in time, I may or may not have told the universe to go fuck itself.

Out loud.

I didn't sleep much at all, and the few times I managed to, I had strange, chaotic dreams that left me disoriented when I woke. Then it took forever for me to get back to sleep, only to have the process repeat itself. By the time my alarm was ready to go off, I knew I'd be depending on lots of caffeine to keep me awake.

Even after two cups of Cuban espresso, I was having a hard time concentrating. It wasn't so bad that anyone really noticed since we were trying to go through things without scripts for the first time, but I could feel that I was a bit off. When we broke for lunch, Todd followed me to where I'd left my purse and coat.

"What's going on?"

Okay, so someone had noticed.

"Weird weekend," I said as I pulled on my coat.

"Do you have lunch plans?"

I shook my head.

He held out his arm. "Then you and I are going to go somewhere quiet so you can tell me all about this weird weekend, and what has your pretty little head all messed up."

I hooked my arm through his, too tired to argue. And if I was being completely honest, I didn't really want to. I was tired, emotionally as well as physically. After having met Dax's mother yesterday, I felt guilty even thinking about going to Carrie with any of this. She didn't need to be reassuring me when I wasn't even sure I deserved to be feeling much of anything at all. Todd was different. He wasn't just a friend. He didn't have any personal stake in this, which meant he could help me figure out whatever the hell it was I needed to figure out.

There was a quiet little bakery around the corner from the theater, a short enough walk that we barely had enough time to get cold despite the brutal wind. Rich smells greeted us when we stepped inside. Cinnamon, fresh bread, various cheeses. Garlic, basil. Other spices I couldn't name. All sorts of different ones that shouldn't have smelled so great together. Then there were the soups. French onion. Tomato. And according to the posted menu, wedding soup was the special today. A wonderful cacophony of aromas.

My stomach growled, and I remembered how long it had been since I'd eaten anything substantial. The two of us were the only ones there, so we went straight to the front. My mouth started to water as I followed Todd to a table near the window less than ten minutes later. I'd probably gotten too much food, but it all looked so good.

I was halfway through an amazingly gooey cinnamon roll before I finally slowed down and let myself start to relax a bit. I hadn't realized how much I needed to eat. I'd never been the sort of girl who starved herself so she could fit into some unrealistic mold. I was the kind who responded to stress by not eating...except when food was this amazing.

"All right, Bryne, time to start talking." Todd dipped a chunk of seven-grain bread into his soup. "What's going on? You're all over the place."

I sighed. "Dax and I went out to eat Tuesday after rehearsal. Then to a movie." I glanced up, then back down to my plate. "And then we went to a hotel."

"Did he force you?"

Todd's voice was tight, his expression tense as my head jerked up to look at him.

"No, of course not. He wouldn't do that." I might not

know Dax well, but he was consistent when it came to making sure I was okay with whatever we were doing.

Todd's expression eased. "Was the sex bad?"

I rolled my eyes. "Seriously? You go from him forcing me, to the sex being bad?"

"So it wasn't?"

I glared at him. "No, Todd, it wasn't bad. It was amazing. Toe-curling, in fact."

"Then what did he do?"

I went through the whole thing, including what I hadn't told Carrie and Annabeth. Things like the completely mixed up way I felt about what was happening with Dax.

"So you still don't know where he is?" Todd asked when I was finally done.

"Nope." The word left a bitter taste in my mouth. "And I don't even feel like I have the right to be pissed when he hasn't even called his mom."

"Do you care about him?"

I leaned forward, resting my head on my hands. I could feel Todd's eyes on me and knew he'd wait for an answer. "Yes, but it's not like I really have any idea what that means. Like I said before, he's the first guy I've ever been with."

"Hon, it doesn't matter if he's the first guy or the twenty-seventh guy." Todd's voice was gentle. "When you know, you know."

I looked up. "I told you about my grandma, how she thought she was in love with Chauncey Manning, and then he left her. Didn't even care that she was pregnant. She never got over it. She might've known how she felt, but he apparently didn't get the memo."

"Do you think it would've made a difference to how she felt if she'd known he'd leave?"

"I don't think she would've slept with him," I said.

"It might've changed her actions, but do you think it would've changed how she felt?"

I took a moment to consider the question. I'd never had a close relationship with my mom's parents. Grandma had never forgiven Mom for marrying a boxer instead of trying to "make something of herself." I'd always thought it was a bit hypocritical of her since my parents had married for love. They'd been poor, but they'd stayed together and in love until the day he died. As I'd gotten older and found out more about the circumstances surrounding my mom's conception, I realized that Grandma had been jealous of what my mom had. No matter what her motivations were though, it meant I didn't have much of a relationship with my grandmother.

But that didn't mean I couldn't put myself in her place. How would I feel if I found out that Dax had just blown me off completely? If he'd contacted his mom some time yesterday and told her that he didn't want me to know where he was? Would I regret the time I'd had with him if this was how things ended? If I discovered that the man I'd given myself to wasn't the man I thought he was?

Even if all of that happened, I might regret having slept with him, but I didn't think it would change how I felt. Confused, yes, but I couldn't deny that there was something far more complicated than I liked going on here.

"I can't think straight around him," I confessed softly. "I mean it's like my brain completely short-circuits when it comes to him. In my head, I know we're supposed to be casual and that it's not a good idea to get involved with him. Then I see him, and all I want..."

I let the statement trail off.

"All you want is to jump his bones?"

I laughed, grateful for the break in tension. "Yeah, that's about right. And trust me, if you'd had sex with him, that's all you'd want to do too."

He joined in my laughter but had a question at the end of it. "But it's not only sex, is it?"

I shook my head. "It'd be easier if that's all it was."

"Tell me about it," Todd said, rolling his eyes. "Sometimes sex makes things more complicated, but there are times when it's a lot simpler when that's all there is to worry about."

I finally let myself voice one of the things that had been worrying me. "Am I going too fast? I mean, I understand that I can't control my feelings for him, but am I rushing something that shouldn't be rushed?"

Todd raised an eyebrow. "Didn't you sleep with him like two days after you guys met?"

I flipped up my middle finger as he laughed. "I'm not talking about the physical part of it. I'd already been thinking about casual sex instead of relationships before I even got here, so I went into that with my eyes wide open."

"You mean emotionally."

I nodded. "Maybe I'm not wired to have sex with no strings attached, or maybe it's just him. What I do know is that every time I'm with him, he gets deeper."

The fact that Todd didn't focus on my unintentional innuendo told me that he understood that I was being serious.

"So you're asking if I think you need to back off so you

don't get any more emotionally involved than you already are."

"Pretty much."

"And you want my advice?"

I gave him a wry look. "As long as it's not to follow my heart, go for it."

"It's out of your hands right now," he said, looking at me with so much sympathy and caring that tears pricked my eyes. "There's nothing you can do except wait for Dax to make his move. Either he'll show up and give you some excuse about what he's been doing so you can decide whether or not to forgive his ass. Or you'll hear that he's being a bastard, and you can move on."

I dropped my face in my hands. "So your great advice is to do nothing?"

He pulled them away, clasping them between his own. "My advice is to focus on what you have right in front of you, and if the shit hits the fan, know that I'll be there to kick his ass if you need me."

It was good advice. I'd been trying to put everything with Dax out of my head, but it hadn't been working at all. Now that I'd spoken to Todd about it, admitted the reality of the feelings I was struggling with, I felt lighter. Not really better, since I still didn't know that he was okay, but lighter.

The feeling stayed with me as Todd and I walked back to the theater. We arrived at the same time as August Dumont, the other male actor in *Collide*. He was attractive, in a rough sort of way. Not like Dax with his tattoos and piercings, but more like those athletes who just had so much charisma that it took them to a different level. Appropriate since he was portraying a baseball player whose career was ruined by the same tragedy that brought the five of us together. Since the script didn't say what that tragedy was, we'd been discussing it among ourselves since the first day. Earlier today, August had joked about us keeping track of all of our ideas.

"Ready to get back to it?" August asked as he fell in step next to me.

"I am." I was surprised to find myself answering honestly.

"She's just looking forward to making out with me," Todd said with a wink.

"Yeah, that's it," I said dryly.

"I think you're the lucky one, Todd." August bumped his elbow against my shoulder. At six and a half feet, his shoulder was too far above mine for me to reach with my elbow.

"Thanks." I gave him a stiff smile.

August was nice enough, and he'd made it clear that he was interested in seeing me outside of work, but it hadn't even been a consideration. Aside from the reasoning I'd given him – that I didn't plan on dating anyone I worked with – I wasn't attracted to him. There was no spark between us, no heat. It hadn't stopped him from flirting, but he wasn't being obnoxious about it, so it didn't bother me.

Part of me wondered what Dax would do if he saw me with August. He'd acted like he was jealous of Todd, who wasn't even interested in me that way. Seeing August hitting on me should make Dax even more possessive, and the thought made something primal in me twist. I'd liked feeling claimed by him, and I now realized that should've been my first clue that I wasn't as indifferent to how things were going as I wanted to believe.

Then again, if Dax was trying to blow me off, he wouldn't care about August at all.

That thought didn't sit well with me, but I reminded myself that I had a job here and that Todd was right. Until Dax decided to make a move, I couldn't do anything about the situation. What I had control over, what I *could* do was become Gretchen and focus on the dream that had brought me to New York in the first place.

End of preview.
Club Prive continues in *Enticed (Club Prive Book 12),* available now.

ABOUT THE AUTHOR

M. S. Parker is a USA Today Bestselling author and the author of the Erotic Romance series, Club Privè and Chasing Perfection.

Living in Las Vegas, she enjoys sitting by the pool with her laptop writing on her next spicy romance.

Growing up all she wanted to be was a dancer, actor or author. So far only the latter has come true but M. S. Parker hasn't retired her dancing shoes just yet. She is still waiting for the call for her to appear on Dancing With The Stars.

When M. S. isn't writing, she can usually be found reading– oops, scratch that! She is always writing.

For more information:
www.msparker.com
msparkerbooks@gmail.com

 facebook.com/msparkerauthor

ACKNOWLEDGMENTS

First, I would like to thank all of my readers. Without you, my books would not exist. I truly appreciate each and every one of you.

A big "thanks" goes out to all the Facebook fans, street team, beta readers, and advanced reviewers. You are a HUGE part of the success of all my series.

I have to thank my PA, Shannon Hunt. Without you my life would be a complete and utter mess. Also a big thank you goes out to my editor Lynette and my wonderful cover designer, Sinisa. You make my ideas and writing look so good.